What Teens A

DIARY OF A TEEN

"I think *Meant to Be* and the whole Diary series are wonderful. I enjoyed reading them so much, and I feel like I am friends with the characters."—HEATHER

"I laughed, I cried...and I believed. I hope you make more Diary of a Teenage Girl series and another chick whose going through the same stuff all of us are."—SAMMY

"Melody Carlson has done it again. The trials and tribulations Kim faces in *Just Ask* remind me of my own life. This is a must-read!"—SARAH

"*Just Ask* shows the amazing works of God in a realistic teenage lifestyle."—ASHLEY

"These are the greatest books of all time! They've really gotten me thinking about my relationship with God. Melody Carlson totally understands us girls, and I fully respect that!"—MORGAN

"*Becoming Me* shined the light on some things that I have been trying to figure out for a long time now and helped me see some things that I couldn't see before."—ELIZABETH

"*My Name Is Chloe* was awesome! I love how God was laced into everything that happened. I couldn't wait to read the second one, and now I can't wait to read the third one!"—EMILY

"I couldn't believe how easy it was to relate Chloe to myself; it was really weird. But then I realized there was nothing weird about it...it was God. God used *Sold Out* to pull me back to Him, and I couldn't be more thankful."—MEGAN

"*Sold Out* is so totally cool, mostly because of how real it is. I love this book!"—CATI

"This series of books are the best books I have ever read. I have never liked to read, but one day my friend told me about *I Do*, and I LOVED it. I could not put this book down."—KIMBERLY

"The Diary of a Teenage Girl series is like no other I have read. I just finished *It's My Life* and absolutely loved it! I feel like this girl, Caitlin O'Conner, is living my life. I look forward to reading the rest of the books in the series."—CAROLYN

"I feel so free when I read this series! It's absolutely so intriguing, fun to read, exciting, emotional, and sad all at the same time! You don't know what to expect when you turn the next page. All my friends are already hooked on this series!—MEGAN

Diary of a Teenage Girl

Kim Book No. 2

Meant to Be

a novel

MELODY CARLSON

MULTNOMAH
BOOKS

MEANT TO BE
published by Multnomah Books
and in association with the literary agency of Sara A. Fortenberry

International Standard Book Number: 978-1-59052-322-3

Cover design by Studiogearbox.com
Cover image by Stephen Gardner, PixelWorkStudio.net

Published in the United States by WaterBrook Multnomah, an imprint of the Crown Publishing Group, a division of Penguin Random House LLC, New York.

Printed in the United States of America

For information:
MULTNOMAH BOOKS
12265 ORACLE BOULEVARD, SUITE 200
COLORADO SPRINGS, CO 80921

Library of Congress Cataloging-in-Publication Data

Carlson, Melody.
Meant to be : a novel / Melody Carlson.
p. cm. — (Diary of a teenage girl. Kim ; bk. 2)
Summary: In spite of a newfound faith, sixteen-year-old Kim Peterson faces a dreary Christmas and New Year because her mother has been diagnosed with cancer.
ISBN 1-59052-322-9
[1. Cancer—Fiction. 2. Korean Americans—Fiction. 3. Mothers—Fiction. 4. Christian life—Fiction. 5. Diaries–Fiction.] I. Title.
PZ7.C216637Mea 2005
[Fic]—dc22

2005014376

15—10 9 8 7 6 5

Books by Melody Carlson:

Piercing Proverbs

DIARY OF A TEENAGE GIRL SERIES

Caitlin O'Conner:

Becoming Me

It's My Life

Who I Am

On My Own

I Do!

Chloe Miller:

My Name Is Chloe

Sold Out

Road Trip

Face the Music

Kim Peterson:

Just Ask

Meant to Be

Falling Up

TRUE COLOR SERIES

Dark Blue, color me lonely

Deep Green, color me jealous

Torch Red, color me torn

Pitch Black, color me lost

Burnt Orange, color me wasted

Fool's Gold, color me consumed

Blade Silver, color me scarred

Bitter Rose, color me broken

One

Saturday, December 17

Christmas break started today. Wait a minute, let's make that winter break. It's the latest controversy around here. Do we call the activities during this time of year "Christmas" or "winter"? For some reason it's got everybody worked up. And unfortunately winter seems to be winning.

Same thing happened with our orchestra concert last week. I mean, I've always called it the Christmas Concert since we play mostly Christmas music. But this year it was officially changed to the Winter Concert in order for the school to be more politically correct and avoid any civil lawsuits. Yeah, right. They even had to reprint the posters, and at no small expense either. The only consolation was that we still played some real Christmas tunes including "Silent Night." Although I hear that may all change by next year.

Well, okay, I suppose it's not the end of civilization as we know it, and it's not like I want to offend some minority religious group, but the truth is, it does irk me a little. I mean, here I am actually celebrating the real reason for the season this year—since I'm a real Christian now—and it seems that everyone else is trying to strip the word "Christmas" off of everything.

I suppose Hallmark will start marketing winter cards to send to all your friends. "Merry Winter, hope you and yours stay warm and dry this season." The ironic thing is that last Christmas, back when I truly believed I was a born-again Buddhist, this kind of absurdity would've made me extremely happy. Now, it just makes me sad.

Okay, that's not the only reason I'm sad. I'm mostly sad about Mom's diagnosis of ovarian cancer. It's like I can feel this gloomy cloud hanging over our entire house now. Although if anyone had been watching my mom these past few days, I'm sure no one would guess that anything is wrong. She's like Mrs. Santa—baking cookies and nut breads, decorating the house, and wrapping packages as if...well, as if it's her last Christmas.

Even writing those words right now puts a huge lump in my throat, and I can't believe it's true. I keep telling myself maybe it's not. Maybe there's been a mistake, a misdiagnosis. Or maybe it's just going to go away.

For the past couple of weeks, I've gone online regularly trying to read up on the latest treatments for the kind of cancer my mom has, and while most of the news is rather dismal, I have discovered a few encouraging stories. And I do believe it's possible that my mom could survive this thing. At least I try to believe it. Sometimes I get pretty depressed.

"Everyone in my church is praying for your mom," Natalie assured me at school yesterday when she noticed I was feeling down. "And a lot of people have sent word out to their online prayer chains, which could mean that literally thousands of people are praying for her right now." Her blue eyes got bigger. "Do you have any idea what that means, Kim?"

I didn't say anything. I guess I was just feeling too bummed to respond intelligently.

"It means that God could do a real miracle!"

"I know," I finally said. "It's just hard sometimes...to believe, you know?"

"But I thought you said your mom is feeling better now, and that she even believes she's going to be healed."

I nodded. "Yeah, I guess she does. I mean, her spirits are up, and she's acting perfectly normal..."

"So you need to do the same thing. For her sake, you need to at least act like you believe she'll be healed, Kim. And maybe it's one of those faith things. Our pastor was talking about that last week. Like when Abraham stepped out into the desert and when Moses stepped into the Red Sea—it was all about faith. But they had to take that first step, and then God stepped in and did the miracle. You know what I mean?"

And suddenly I sort of did understand what she meant. "Yeah," I finally said. "Maybe that's what my mom's doing now—taking that step of faith."

"And you need to do it too. We all have to believe this for her, Kim. We have to expect a miracle. Who knows, maybe it will happen at Christmas. Can you imagine how cool that would be?"

And so for a while at school, I really did feel somewhat encouraged, and I really did believe that God could and would do a miracle for my mom. I was being really positive when I got home too. And I told Mom that I believed she was going to be healed. She just smiled and nodded like she believed it too. And everything was pretty cool.

Then this morning, I went online again. I visited some new medical websites, which turned out to have some less-than-happy facts, and now I'm feeling all discouraged again. The stupid thing is, I only went online to pick out some letters for my Just Ask Jamie column. Instead I ended up spending the whole morning getting thoroughly depressed. So much for my big step of faith, huh?

Anyway, I finally quit searching the web for miracles and went to my e-mail box, reading the most recent letters that had been forwarded to me from the newspaper. I'm supposed to be looking for something that specifically pertains to Christmas, since Dad suggested I focus next week's column on Christmas, and I finally found a couple that will work.

Dear Jamie,

I'm feeling really torn. My parents got divorced a few years ago, and they both want me to spend Christmas with them this year. My dad recently remarried and just invited me to go on a very cool skiing vacation in Aspen, Colorado, with him and his new wife and her kids—which sounds totally awesome. But then my mom would be all alone, and she's already kind of depressed, so I feel sort of bad about leaving her behind. What should I do?

Guilt Ridden

Dear Guilt Ridden,

I think you already know the answer to your question. But let me ask you a question—what does Christmas really mean to you? Have you heard about the baby who left His Father's glorious kingdom to be born in a drafty old barn and into a family that was considered "peasant class"? That was the first Christmas...and it was about things like love and sacrifice and mercy. I guess the real question is, what kind of Christmas do you want to celebrate this year?

Just Jamie

Okay, I hope that wasn't too harsh. I know my dad is expecting "uplifting" responses, but honestly, that letter just got to me. I mean, how could this person (not sure if it's a guy or girl) even consider ditching a hurting parent to go off to enjoy the lifestyles of the rich and famous? It just seems all wrong.

What I really wanted to ask was, how would you feel if you knew your mother was dying? What if this was your last Christmas to be with her? Of course, I can't write that. And I'm probably imposing my own situation onto this poor person who's just writing to ask for advice, when I should be asking myself these questions.

How would I feel if I knew this was Mom's last Christmas with us? And can I even face the answer? The truth is, this is tearing me apart.

TWO

Monday, December 19

"Want to do some Christmas shopping with me?" my mom asks as I pour myself a cup of coffee and try to make my eyes open wide enough to see clearly. I've barely crawled out of bed, and I'm really not ready for any conversation yet. Still, this is Mom. I can't just ignore her.

"When?" I ask.

"This morning. Maybe we could leave early enough to avoid some of the last-minute shopping rush. Then we could have a nice lunch together, just the two of us."

Okay, I already told Matthew that I'd go ice skating with him at noon today. He's never been, and I promised that I'd teach him. But instead of telling Mom about my plans, I agree to go shopping with her. Then when I'm in my room, I call and leave a message on Matthew's cell phone.

"Sorry, I won't be able to go skating with you today," I say not wanting to go into the full explanation. "Uh, something came up. Do you think we could do it tomorrow instead? Let me know."

I believe it's the right thing to spend time with my mom, but I also feel a little bummed about canceling on Matthew like that. He was so excited about learning how to skate—it was cute the way he was worried about falling down and making a fool of himself. I can't believe he's never even gone before, and I'd really looked forward to this. I just hope he doesn't think I'm blowing him off. Especially considering that I've been a little chilly to him lately. But that's only because I've been so distracted by this thing with my mom. He should be able to understand that. Shouldn't he?

"I thought you were all done with Christmas shopping," I say as I back my Jeep out of the driveway. It's really surprising how comfortable my mom has gotten about my driving lately, but then I guess in light of everything else...well, she's probably not that worried about fender benders anymore.

"I thought so too, but then I remembered a couple of things." She leans back into the seat and sighs.

I glance at her. "You okay?"

She smiles. "Yes, I feel perfectly fine. I was just thinking what a beautiful day this is—so sunny and bright. Only it doesn't look like there's much chance of having a white Christmas this year."

"You never know..." I say hopefully. I've always been

such a sucker for snow. I used to actually pray for snow every Christmas when I was little—before I gave up on God and turned to Buddha. I could pray for snow this year now that I'm a believer again, but then I have way more important things to pray for now. I don't plan on wasting God's time on something as silly as snow.

When we get to the mall, there is tinny sounding Christmas music playing a little too loudly, a long line of impatient-looking kids waiting to see Santa, and lots and lots of last-minute shoppers hurrying around. Mom isn't moving too fast, but she seems to know where she's going, and it looks like she's heading straight for Dolman's jewelry store. Now I think this is kind of strange, but I just go along with her.

"I wanted to get your dad something special," she tells me as we go inside the formal-looking store where the music is quieter and more classical sounding.

We walk up to a long glass case. "What's that?"

"It's something he's always wanted, but I guess I never got around to finding one."

"What?" I'm suddenly feeling pretty curious since Dad has never been the kind of guy who's into jewelry. I mean, I certainly can't imagine him wearing gold chains or any other form of bling-bling for that matter.

"A pocket watch."

"Really?"

"Yes." She pauses at a watch counter and looks down at all the shiny wristwatches. "His father had one that his father had given him. But he lost it on a fishing trip when Dad was a boy, and your father always felt like he missed out on something."

"Interesting..." I lean over the counter and look too, but I don't see any pocket watches, and I'm actually wondering if people even make them anymore.

"Can I help you?" asks a tall redheaded saleswoman. I can't help but notice that this lady is dripping in diamonds: on her fingers, her wrist, around her neck. Even her ears are pierced several times, and each hole is sporting a diamond. I wonder if they're real and if they all belong to her or if she's just wearing them as an advertisement to entice shoppers. And if they do belong to her, why is she working as a salesclerk? Don't they just make minimum wage? Or maybe she owes her soul to the company store and will be working here to pay for her diamonds until she's an old lady.

"I'm looking for a pocket watch," my mom says almost apologetically. "Do you have any?"

The diamond woman smiles. "Not many, but we do have a few. They're down this way." She leads us to the end of the counter where she bends down and then pulls out a velvet-covered tray displaying about six different pocket watches.

I pick up a gold one with a red stone set in the center. "This one is cool," I tell Mom. Then I flip it over to see the price tag and am pretty surprised at the cost. Mom is looking at a silver one that I'm guessing is less expensive.

"That's pretty," I tell her as I carefully put the gold watch down.

"You have very good taste," says the salesclerk. "That one is platinum."

"Platinum?" I echo. "Isn't that even more expensive than gold?"

She nods. "It's a precious metal like gold but more rare. And it's stronger too. That's important for a pocket watch since it rubs around in a pocket."

"I'll take it," Mom says without even checking the price. I try not to blink or act too shocked. I can't see the price tag from where I'm standing, but I suspect that it must cost even more than the expensive one I just set down. Gulp.

"Can you have it engraved?" my mom asks.

"Certainly," says the pleased salesclerk. "But it won't be ready until tomorrow. Our engraver is a little backed up with Christmas, you know."

"That's all right." Mom follows the woman to the register. Now I'm feeling kind of sick about this. Mom is spending way too much money on this watch, and although I'm not an expert on our family's finances, we're normally pretty frugal. I can't help but think that Mom's doing this because she's worried that this might be her last chance...and it's making me feel seriously freaked.

"Why don't you look around, honey, while I take care of this and fill out the engraving form."

I wander around the jewelry store feeling like a robot that's pretending to look at things but not really seeing anything. Mostly I'm thinking about Mom, trying to figure this thing out.

"Can I help you?" asks a gray-haired salesman.

"Huh?" I attempt to focus.

"Are you shopping for anything specific?"

"Oh, no...I'm just looking."

He smiles. "I know just what you need, young lady."

Now I'm curious. "What?" I ask him, almost as a challenge. "What is it you think I need?"

"Come over here." He leads me to a glass-covered case full of glistening diamonds—pendants and rings and bracelets and earrings. "After all," he says, "diamonds are a girl's best friend."

I sort of roll my eyes as I lean over and look more closely at the sparkling jewelry. And although I've never considered myself a material girl, I am slightly fascinated by all that glitter. I'm trying to imagine what it must all be worth. "That's a lot of diamonds."

"I see that your ears are pierced. You'd look lovely in diamonds."

I kind of laugh. "Yeah, right. I'm only sixteen. Well, almost seventeen. I don't really have the budget for diamonds yet."

"So you haven't considered diamond studs earrings yet? Lots of girls your age wear them."

"I guess I'm waiting until I become rich and famous."

Now my mom comes and stands by me. "Oh my, look at all those pretty diamonds." She bends down to see better.

"We're having a holiday sale," entices the older man,

turning his attention from me to her. "Twenty percent off until Christmas Eve."

She nods and continues looking. This is kind of odd since my mom's not exactly the expensive jewelry type. At least I never thought she was. But maybe I wasn't paying attention.

"I didn't know you were into diamonds," I say to my mom.

"Oh, you two are together," the man says with a surprised look. Of course, I'm used to this reaction—people see the Asian girl with the Caucasian woman and wonder how or if we're related. Anyone out there ever hear of international adoption? Okay, don't get me going.

But Mom just smiles at him and proudly says, "Yes, this is my daughter."

"In that case, I might be tempted to offer an even bigger discount if you both find something you like."

My mom actually giggles, which is really kind of cute. "Oh, no, I'm not a diamond sort of person. Well, other than my engagement ring." She looks fondly at her left hand. "But Kim, how about you? Do you like diamonds?"

"I, uh—"

"I was just telling the young lady that she should consider some earrings," says the fast-thinking salesman.

"Yes, diamond earrings! That would be perfect!"

"Mom?" I look at her as if I'm looking at a stranger. "You don't need to—"

"Can we look at that tray?" My mom points to a display of earrings and ignores me.

He pulls out the tray while I protest to my mom about the extravagance of diamond earrings for a girl my age.

"Please, Kim," she finally says. "Just indulge me."

This makes the man laugh. "Yes, Kim, just indulge her."

Before I know it I am trying on diamond earrings, and despite myself I am having fun. And as much as I hate to admit it, it does feel rather glamorous.

"Okay," Mom says after I've looked at several pairs. "You go out into the mall while I make up my mind."

"Mom? I thought we were just having fun."

She looks at me then smiles. "I thought that's what we were doing too. Now, you scoot."

Okay, I have no doubts that she's getting me diamond earrings for Christmas, and as exciting and fun as that sounds, it also makes me seriously uncomfortable. Like why is she doing this? Why is she spending so much money when she usually clips coupons and buys us practical gifts for Christmas? But I know I can't make too big of a deal about it—not without the risk of spoiling her fun anyway. And I don't want to do that.

She emerges with a big grin, and I pretend like I have no idea what just transpired in there.

We do a bit more shopping, but I can tell Mom's getting tired, so I ask her if she's ready to eat lunch yet.

"Yes. Let's go to Rafael's."

"Rafael's? What? Did you win the lottery or something?"

"Oh, Kimmy. It's okay to indulge ourselves occasionally."

"But you don't have to do this for—"

"I want to, Kim. Can't you see that I'm having a good time? I just want to enjoy this day, sweetheart. Do you mind?"

I shake my head. "Of course not. I'd love to go to Rafael's. I've heard it's awesome. But do you think we need reservations or anything?"

"I doubt it. At least not during the day."

So we head back out to the parking lot, and I drive us over to the other side of the mall where you can only get into this restaurant from an outside entrance. "This is really cool, Mom." I hold the door open for her.

The restaurant has soft music playing and small tables with pristine white cloths, as well as candles and fresh flowers on each one. Very elegant.

Soon we are seated, and I must admit that I'm feeling pretty special. I mean, diamond earrings and Rafael's all in one day. But even though this is fun, I can't help but feel that it's all overshadowed by Mom's recent diagnosis. I'm certain we wouldn't be doing this if everything was just fine. And the truth is, I would gladly trade diamonds and Rafael's for "just fine" any day.

After the waiter takes our orders, my mom tells me that she "wants to talk." And I can tell by the way she says this that this is somewhat serious. And suddenly I feel as if there's a brick in the pit of my stomach, and I doubt that I'll be able to eat a single bite.

"Sure, Mom," I say, trying to sound casual. "What about?"

"About us." She takes a sip of water. "I just want to set some things straight, Kim. Okay?"

"Okay."

"I realize that you're worried about me and, well, the cancer. But I really wish that you could just push it out of your mind."

"Push it out of my mind?"

She nods. "That's what I'm trying to do. I'm focusing on health and wellness. I'm doing everything I can, and I want to just enjoy life. Whether I live to be a hundred or buy the farm next week. Can you understand that?"

"Well, yeah, I guess..."

"And that's how I want you to live too. I don't want you to change anything because of me. Do you understand what I mean?"

"I'm not sure."

"I want you to go about your life as if everything is normal, Kim. And for all we know, it is. Right?"

I remember what Natalie told me about how I need to take the step of faith with my mom in order to encourage her. So I say, "Right."

"Like you've been saying, Kim, God can heal me. Don't you believe that?"

"Yes," I say with a bit more enthusiasm. "I do believe

that He can. And I'm praying, and lots of people are praying."

She smiles now. "See that's just what I mean. We need to believe that God's in control of our lives and not to worry so much."

"I know..."

"And I want you to make me a promise, Kim."

"What?"

"Promise me that you'll keep doing all your normal things—whether it's spending time with Nat or your music or your column or even spending time with Matthew. Promise me that everything will continue to be 'life as normal.' Can you do that for me?"

I slowly nod. "Okay."

"Because that's what will make me the most happy. Do you believe me?"

I nod again, holding back tears. And I really do believe her. But for the first time I realize that I must've been bringing her down by moping around these past few weeks. I thought I was concealing it pretty well, but I guess she saw right through my little charade. From now on, I will put on a happy and faithful face. And I'll pray and pray and pray. Maybe this is what Nat meant by taking that first step. I can do this. I force myself to eat, as if everything is perfectly normal and I'm not worried about a thing.

We have a good lunch, and Mom actually begins to open up and tell me about things that happened when she was my age. It's the first time I've ever heard her talk about stuff like that, and I must admit that it's pretty interesting. I mean, I guess I never thought about Mom being a teenager. It's like I think she's always been this rather conservative middle-aged woman I've taken pretty much for granted. But as she tells me about the time she participated in an antiwar protest at her college, I can see that I really don't know her as well as I thought.

"Seriously?" I say as we indulge in calorie-laden desserts. "You were a war protester?"

She smiles and nods. "I never thought we should've been in Vietnam."

"Wow, that's pretty cool. Did you get arrested?"

She laughs now. "No, but I was willing to go to jail and was actually kind of disappointed that I didn't."

So, go figure!

Later on that evening, after I'd talked to Matthew, assured him that I still wanted to go skating, and promised that we'd do it tomorrow, I decided that I'd better crank out another "Christmas" letter for the column. After going through the pile I found this.

Dear Jamie,

My little brother is five years old and was acting like a typical little brat yesterday, and I got so irritated at him that I told him there was no Santa Claus, and I went on and on about it. Well, you should've seen his face—it was like I'd murdered someone. Now I feel really guilty and don't know what to do. Any suggestions?

Santa Spoiler

Dear Spoiler,

Since your little brother is only five, it might be possible to undo this. Why not just tell him that it was only because of your anger that you told him Santa was a fake? Tell him that you were just trying to make him feel bad and then tell him you're sorry—since that's actually the truth. And maybe this will help him to understand that people sometimes say mean things when they're feeling irritated. Hopefully he'll forgive you and get to enjoy the whole Santa thing for a little longer.

Just Jamie

Three

Friday, December 23

I've spent this week doing "normal" things, trying to act as if everything is just fine and I'm not the least bit worried about Mom. It was hard at first, and I found myself wanting to make up excuses just to hang out at home and stay close to Mom. But then I'd remind myself of the promise I'd made her at Rafael's, and because of that, I went ahead and forced myself to do regular stuff with my friends.

On Tuesday, I went ice skating with Matthew, and it was really pretty fun. He fell down about a zillion times, and I was certain he was going to break something before we were done. But he finally got the hang of it and actually liked it. We're going to go again next week, maybe invite some friends.

But the whole while I was skating with Matthew and mostly enjoying myself, I had this nagging guilty feeling...like I shouldn't be having so much fun or I should leave and go home to be with my mom. And I suppose that took some of the fun out of the day. But when I got home, my mom was just fine, and she seemed really glad that I'd had a fun day. And Matthew came in and visited and chowed down about a dozen Christmas cookies, and everything felt almost normal.

As the week progressed, it became easier to go and do regular stuff, but there's always this underlying feeling that something's wrong. Like I shouldn't be out having a good time. Then I remember my promise.

"Did you get Matthew anything for Christmas?" my mom asked me last night.

Now for some reason this idea hadn't even crossed my mind. I mean, I like Matthew, and we've sort of been dating, although it's not serious. But suddenly I wondered if I should've gotten him something. And if so, what?

"No," I told my mom, acting like it was no big deal. "We're mostly just friends, you know."

She nodded as if she understood, but when I went to my room, I immediately called Nat and asked her opinion on the matter.

"I don't know..." she began.

"It's not like we're serious or anything."

"Yeah. And you might feel stupid if you got him something and he acted all surprised and uncomfortable, like he hadn't gotten you anything."

I considered this. "That would be pretty embarrassing."

"On the other hand..."

"What if he got me something?"

"Yeah," she said. "That could be awkward."

"Maybe I should get a kind of back-up gift in case he does get me something," I said. "Then I could pull it out and look like I had it together too."

"But you wouldn't have to give it to him if he didn't get you anything."

"Right."

"The back-up gift," Nat said in a dramatic tone.

"You sound like a 'Seinfeld' character," I teased.

So that's why Nat and I made the fateful decision to hit the mall just two days before Christmas. And man, was the place packed! When we walked past Dolman's, I couldn't help but spill the beans on what my mom had gotten for Christmas.

"No way," said Nat. "You're getting diamond earrings?"

"Well, I'm not positively sure. But there's a pretty good chance."

"You are so lucky." Then a shadow crossed her face, as if she'd suddenly remembered about my mom's cancer. But fortunately she didn't mention it, and I told her about the pocket watch for my dad.

"That's so romantic."

"So what should I get for Matthew?" I looked both ways down the crowded mall.

"What does he like?"

I shrugged. "I guess I really don't know him that well.

Other than art. Oh, he likes science fiction books, but I have no idea which ones he's read. And I know what music groups he likes, but I don't know what CDs he has. Plus he thinks he's getting an MP3 player for Christmas."

"How about some art stuff?"

"Yeah. And I could get something that I like just in case I don't need the back-up gift."

"Or else save the receipt and bring it back later."

"Great plan, Nat."

So it is that I get Matthew a sketch pad, some charcoal, pencils, and a few other things. He probably has stuff like this already, but I figured it was something he could use eventually since these things run out.

"What did you get your mom for Christmas?" Nat asked when we stopped to get drinks.

"I kind of splurged," I admitted. An understatement since most of my Christmas shopping money went for this one gift.

"What?" she demanded.

"Cashmere."

"No way!"

I nodded. "Yep. I got her a sweater set at Malone's."

"Wow, she's gonna love it. What color?"

"It's kind of a periwinkle."

"Very cool."

I didn't tell Nat that this meant I had to skimp on her gift this year. But I have a feeling she'll understand. Besides, she's been saying that she wanted a photo album, and I even put a few old pictures of her and me in it. Hopefully that will make up for it. And in a way it's probably a good thing, since I know how strapped Nat's been lately. She barely had enough money to get her own family anything for Christmas this year. She'd been hoping her dad would send her some money, but as usual he flaked out on her.

"Hey, isn't that Chloe Miller over there?" Nat said just as I was finishing up my soda.

I glanced over my shoulder to see that she was right. And there were Allie and Laura too. We hollered and waved then hurried over to see our famous friends.

"We just got back from our Christmas tour last night," Chloe said. "Man, it's so great to be home! How are you guys anyway?"

"We're doing great," said Natalie. "It's so totally cool to see you here today."

"I can't believe you decided to fight the crowds at the mall on your first day back home," I said. "If I were you, I'd be home sleeping."

"We had to do some last-minute Christmas shopping." Allie held up several bulging bags.

"How was your tour?" I asked.

"Awesome," Laura said, and then all three of them started telling us about where they'd been and the bands that had performed with them, including Iron Cross, which was actually pretty impressive.

"What a life!" Nat said dreamily.

"Maybe we should become their groupies," I teased

her. "We could follow Redemption all over the country and—"

"That'd be like so totally nuts!" said Allie.

"Yeah," Chloe agreed. "Do you have any idea how exhausting it is to be on the road like that? I mean, parts of it are fun, but there are times when we all would give anything to sleep for a few days."

We talked some more, but I could tell these girls were itching to finish up their shopping, and then they probably wanted to go home to rest. In fact, they all seemed pretty worn out, and Allie had these dark circles beneath her eyes, which got me worried that she might be sick again. She had a pretty hard case of mono last fall, and I wonder if she's really over it yet.

"We should let you guys go," I told them.

"Will we see you at church tomorrow night?" asked Chloe.

"I'm not sure," I admitted. "I mean, I'd really like to be at Faith Fellowship on Christmas Eve, but I should probably go to the service at my parents' church this year."

Then Chloe's face got serious, and she put her hand on my arm. "Oh, Kim, I just remembered. I was so sorry to hear about your mom. Josh e-mailed me about it a couple weeks ago. That's got to be so tough."

"But we've all been praying for her," Laura said hopefully.

"Thanks," I told them. "We're all praying for a miracle."

"God can do it," Allie assured me. "He can do

anything, Kim. We just gotta believe Him." Then we all hugged and went our different ways.

"Those girls are so cool," Nat said as we headed toward the parking lot. "I mean, here they are all rich and famous, and they still just act like regular girls. Just ordinary people like us."

"Yeah, they're pretty cool."

And once we were in my Jeep, I played Redemption's latest CD, and Nat and I listened to it all the way home. They really are good!

"We're heading to my grandma's first thing in the morning," Nat told me when I stopped in front of her house to let her out. "So I probably won't see you until later next week."

"Have a good time," I told her, although she was frowning, and I realized how she really wasn't looking forward to this trip. Her grandma and mom get into it sometimes, and I've heard their family gatherings can get kind of stressful.

"Well, at least Gram has a computer now." She reached for her purse. "Maybe I can e-mail you all the gory details."

I laughed. "Yeah, keep me posted. Merry Christmas!"

"Yeah, back at you!" she yelled as she closed the door and headed up the driveway where her little brother Micah was trying to skateboard but looked more like an accident waiting to happen.

So I reminded myself to pray for Nat and her family as I drove down the street toward my house. I mean, she's been praying for my mom to get well on a daily basis, but it hardly ever occurs to me to be praying for them, and I know that they have it pretty tough.

I was kind of glad that Nat and I had already exchanged our gifts, agreeing not to open them until Christmas. Not that I'm embarrassed by what I got her, but I guess it's not as impressive as most years. I hope she understands.

When I got inside, the house was quiet and dark. This worried me some, and I instantly imagined that something was wrong—like maybe Mom got sick and Dad had to take her to the hospital. So I went straight to the kitchen and looked on the counter for a note. But the fact that nothing was there actually concerned me more, like maybe they didn't have time to write a note. I paced around for a while then finally decided to call Dad's cell.

"Hi, sweetheart," he says calmly, as if everything's just fine.

"Where are you guys?"

"Sorry, Kim. We should've let you know we were going, but I caught your mom off guard this afternoon. I got off work early and came in and swept her away with me. You don't mind, do you?"

I know I should be relieved that everything's okay, but I'm feeling a little irked. "I guess not. But it would've been nice if you left a note."

He laughs. "Seems like I've heard that one before, Kimmy, but it's usually coming from me or your mom. Guess you know how we feel now."

"Yeah, right."

"We'll be back in a half an hour or so. Maybe we'll stop off and get a pizza to bring home. You going to be home tonight? No big dates or anything?"

I laugh sarcastically. "No, Dad, no big dates."

"Got your New Year's column all ready to go yet?"

"That's not due until Tuesday," I remind him.

"But we might be out of town," he says in a mysterious voice.

"Out of town?"

"Yeah, we'll tell you more when we get home. In the meantime, you might want to get your New Year's column done just in case."

So I go up to my computer and pull up several letters that might possibly be answered in a way that pertains to New Year's.

Dear Jamie,

I'm so lonely I think I'm going to die. My best friend moved away last summer, and I haven't made a single friend since then. All I do is stay home and watch TV, day after day after day, and I can't stand it anymore. And at the same time, it's like I'm so totally freaked about making a friend that I'm paralyzed. Help!!!

Lonely Girl

Dear Lonely Girl,

I think it's time for you to make a New Year's resolution—and that is to MAKE A FRIEND! The only way to make a friend is to make sure that you're ready to BE a friend. And the way you do that is by making the decision, right now, that you will step out of your comfort zone and get to know someone. You asked for help—here it is. On your first day back at school, you must decide to keep your eyes wide open, and you must look for a girl who's also in need of a friend. Then you must approach her and try to start up a conversation—maybe you'll compliment her on her outfit or hair or whatever. If that doesn't work, don't feel bad. You just have to try it again with someone else. And you might have to do it again and again and again until you make a friend. If you can't find a friend at school, try church. But don't give up. And don't let yourself off the hook until you've made at least one good friend.

Just Jamie

Dear Jamie,

I started hanging with a new bunch of friends this fall. The partying kids, if you know what I mean. I thought it was so cool at first; I mean, that they would want me around. But now I'm starting to realize that all they want to do is get stoned or drunk all the time, and I guess I'm a little worried that it might not be such a great idea. Also, I'm worried that I might get in trouble with my parents or even the law. But at the same time, I don't want to miss out on all the fun either. And I really like some of these kids because they are kind of fun. What should I do?

Party Chick

Dear Party Chick,

I think it's time for you to make a New Year's resolution too. You are exactly right to be worried about getting into trouble. Drugs and underage drinking can: 1) get you arrested, 2) cause a car wreck, 3) make you seriously ill, 4) make you do something you wouldn't normally do, 5) get you grounded for a really long time, or 6) get you or someone else hurt or even killed. Need I say more? It's time for you to just say no to your party friends. And while you're at it, do like Lonely Girl (above) and make some NEW friends too. Maybe even try out a church youth group. But in my opinion it's time to give up the partying before you're really sorry.

Just Jamie

I wonder if kids really listen to the answers in my column or do they just laugh and continue doing what they want? And that's when it occurs to me that I should be praying for these kids. Okay, I don't know their real names, but I suspect that God would understand that.

So I start making a prayer list, and I decide to include not only the kids who get their letters answered in my column, but the other ones too. I put down Nat's family and a few other kids from school, like Marissa and even Matthew since he's not a Christian yet. And suddenly I'm thinking that this is kind of exciting! Of course, I will probably still spend most of my prayer time asking God to heal my mom, but it might be good to be thinking about all these others as well.

Four

Monday, December 26

After a nice quiet Christmas Eve at my parents' church, Dad announced that everything was all set and that we're going to the mountains to stay in his boss's cabin and hopefully get in some skiing for a few days. I'm actually pretty glad because I haven't skied for a while, and last month Cesar talked me into signing up for a youth group snow trip scheduled for January. I almost backed out of it when I found out that Mom was sick, but then my parents decided to pay for it as part of my Christmas present so I guess it's settled.

Now I'm hoping that I'll get in enough practice this week so I won't make a total fool of myself next month. Especially since it's possible that Matthew might go on the youth group trip too. He surprised me by stopping by to wish me a Merry Christmas yesterday.

"Sounds like you're having a pretty nice Christmas

break," Matthew said after I told him about the ski trip my dad had just sprung on us. "I haven't been snowboarding in ages."

"My youth group is having a snow trip," I told him. "It's the weekend after New Year's. You could talk to Cesar about coming on it if you want."

He considered this, and just when I felt certain he was going to blow it off for being a "church" thing, he said he might look into it. Then he handed me what appeared to be a Christmas present.

"What is it?" I said in excited surprise as I examined the smooth, flat package. It was wrapped in pale green paper that appeared to be handmade and tied with raffia and a piece of holly. Quite attractive, really.

He shrugged and looked slightly embarrassed. "Just something I made. Thought you might like it."

"I have something for you too," I said suddenly, racing over to the Christmas tree that was now void of packages except this one. I could tell he was relieved when I handed it to him. I'm sure he probably had the same uncomfortable feeling that I'd experienced when I imagined giving him a gift only to discover that he hadn't done likewise.

So we sat on the couch to open our packages together. I was glad that not only had I taken the time to carefully wrap mine, but I'd also done a little sketch on the first page of the sketchbook, kind of a Christmas scene with a tree and an elflike character saying, "Merry Christmas, Matthew!" Because when I opened my gift I could see that Matthew had put a fair amount of effort into it.

"This is so beautiful." I studied the neatly framed pen and ink drawing. "When did you do this?"

"Last night," he told me.

I looked carefully at the portrait of a mother and small daughter. Although their faces weren't fully shown, it definitely had an Asian feel to it. "It's amazing."

"You really like it?"

I turned to look at him, seeing that he hadn't even opened my package yet. I nodded. "It's awesome, Matthew. I love it."

He smiled. "I saw this photograph in a magazine my mom had, and for some reason it reminded me of you. So I decided to draw it last night. I like how it turned out."

"So do I. I really love it!" Now I looked at the still-unopened package in his lap. "But now my gift seems pretty dull compared to this."

"No," he said quickly as he tore into the package and removed the sketch pad and pencils. "Hey, I needed a new one. Thanks, Kim!"

"It's nothing like this..." I sat staring at the drawing, still impressed with the thought and talent that had gone into it.

"Oh, hello," my mom said as she came into the living room. "I didn't realize you had company, Kim."

"Look at this, Mom!" I got up and took the picture to her. "Matthew drew it."

She peered at the picture for a long moment then looked over at Matthew still sitting on the couch. "That is beautiful, Matthew. Truly beautiful."

"Thanks, Mrs. Peterson." But he looked slightly embarrassed now.

"You're a very good artist, Matthew."

"Thanks."

"We have fresh cinnamon rolls in the kitchen," she said. "And I just made a pot of coffee."

He smiled. "Sounds good."

"Did you have a good Christmas?" she asked him.

He kind of shrugged. "It was okay, I guess."

"Well, it's nice to see you today." Then she turned to me. "Dad went for a walk, and I'm going to take a short nap. The turkey is in the oven now, but it won't be done until around five." She glanced back at Matthew. "Maybe you'd like to join us for dinner later?"

"Man, that sounds good, but I promised my mom I'd be back in time to help her. She invited some relatives over this evening...and, well, you know how that goes."

Mom smiled. "I'm sure it must be nice. We don't have much family around here." Then she headed off to her room, and I led Matthew to the kitchen.

"Where are your parents' families?" he asked as he sat at the counter and reached for a cinnamon roll.

As I poured us some coffee, I told him about my parents' families. "My mom has a few relatives back East, but her parents are both dead. And my dad's family, his older brother and mom, live in Florida. His brother has been having some health problems lately, and Grandma Peterson is getting old, so they don't come to visit much. Mostly it's just the three of us. Pretty quiet."

"Well, that sounds good to me. This whole houseful of feuding relatives thing gets old, especially during the holidays."

I nodded as I handed him a mug of coffee. "It's weird, but Nat kind of said the same thing. And then she e-mailed me this story about her mom and aunt and grandma really getting worked up over a stupid recipe for cornbread. It almost makes me thankful that we don't have a bunch of family around. But then I'd like to think that not all families fight during the holidays."

"I'm sure there must be some happy ones out there." He pulled off a piece of cinnamon roll and popped it in his mouth. "I just don't happen to know of any personally. So when do you guys get back from the mountains?"

"Dad said we leave on Tuesday and stay until Sunday."

"So you'll be gone for New Year's Eve?"

I glanced over at Mom's calendar on the fridge. "Yeah, I guess so."

Now Matthew looked slightly bummed.

"Why?"

"Oh, I was going to invite you to a party."

"What party?" I asked.

"Robert Sanchez is having something..."

My brows rose a bit. Knowing Robert, it would probably be a drinking party. "Oh..."

"He's got a live band and everything."

"Oh..." I said again.

Matthew sighed. "Yeah, I know there's probably going to be alcohol there, Kim. But that doesn't mean you have to get wasted, you know."

I nodded. "I know..."

"But you think it might compromise your convictions," he said in more of a statement than a question.

"I guess so."

"Right." But he didn't look convinced.

"I just don't see why they have to have alcohol at parties," I said. "I mean, don't you remember what a mess it was the night of the Harvest Dance when Marissa and Robert drank too much? Where's the fun in that?"

"Yeah, I can kind of see your point. But that was because Marissa overdid it. And you know how she is; she overdoes everything."

"Maybe, but why even go there in the first place?"

"It's something to do," he said. "A way to celebrate the New Year."

"Well, if I was going to be home that night," I said in a firm voice, "I'd rather go to the skating party that our church is having. Everyone's going to dress up like people from the fifties, and I think that sounds like fun."

He seemed to consider this, and I suddenly

remembered that his mother was a costume designer for our community theater.

"And I'll bet you could come up with a cool outfit, Matthew. Maybe you should go."

He kind of shrugged. "I don't know..."

"If you call Cesar about the ski trip, why not ask him about the skating party too?"

Matthew gave me a mischievous grin. "Why? Are you worried that I'll get plastered at Robert's party?"

"Maybe. Or maybe I just think you'd have more fun doing something else."

"Well, I'll think about it."

We decided to go out and get some fresh air and ended up playing a game of "horse," which I nearly won. Then Dad got home, and we played a quick game of two-on-one basketball (me and Dad against Matthew). But Matthew definitely had the height and not a bad hook shot either.

"You're really good, Matthew," my dad said after Matthew soundly beat us, and we all went inside for a soda. "I'm surprised you don't go out for basketball. From what I'm hearing, Harrison High could use you this year."

"I used to play." He popped open a can and took a long swig.

"Why'd you quit?" I asked, slightly surprised that this long-haired artsy guy had ever been into sports.

"Long story." Matthew took another drink and glanced up at the clock. Then I remembered something he'd told me about his dad once, how he'd really been into sports and had encouraged Matthew when he was younger. But then his parents split up a few years ago, and I suspect that did something to Matthew's interest in sports.

"I should probably go." He handed me the empty soda can. "Thanks for everything." He turned to Dad. "Good game."

Dad laughed. "Good for you anyway."

Then I walked him to the door. "Thanks again for the picture. I really do love it."

He nodded as he pulled on his sweatshirt. "Cool." He paused to look at me. "Those new earrings?"

I smiled. "Yeah. Real diamonds. My mom got them for me for Christmas."

"Wow. They look really pretty on you."

"Thanks. Now don't forget to call Cesar about the ski trip," I reminded him as I opened the front door. I controlled myself from mentioning the New Year's Eve party again. But after I watched his old blue pickup going down the street and turning the corner, I immediately ran back into the house to call Cesar.

After wishing him a Merry Christmas, I told him about Matthew's interest in the ski trip.

"That's cool."

"So I told him to call you. But then I thought maybe you could talk him into going to the skating party too. I'm going to be gone, but I thought Matthew might really enjoy it."

"Great idea, Kim."

"But don't tell him I called," I said quickly. "I mean, I don't want it to sound like I'm planning out his life or anything. I, uh, just care about him, you know?"

"I get you. Matthew's a cool guy. But he needs Jesus."

"Yeah."

"Have fun skiing," he said. "Don't break anything."

I laughed. "Yeah, I'll try to come home in one piece."

Thursday, December 29

Well, I tried snowboarding on my first day here, and after a half day of falling on my face about every thirty seconds, I think I finally got the hang of it. And now I totally love it and have absolutely no desire to go back to skis. Of course, Dad's not too pleased at the idea of renting a board each day (especially since I already have my own skis), but Mom talked him into it.

"Who knows when we'll be up here to do this again?" she said, and he didn't protest. I almost wish he had.

Mom has never been into skiing herself, but Dad's not bad for an old dude, and he's the one who introduced me to the sport in the first place. Even so, I know that Mom loves coming up here. She likes the snow and mountain air, and she brought along her books and knitting and really enjoys sitting by the fire in the lodge or even out on the deck when the sun is shining.

Dad and I made sure that we came in regularly to check on her. But she already seemed to have made a couple of friends with other moms who aren't interested in hitting the slopes either. So we all seemed to be having a pretty good time. And I was becoming a fairly respectable boarder or "rider" as another girl up here told me.

"How long you been riding?" she asked as we rode the blue chairlift together. For the most part, my cautious dad likes to avoid the blue route so I've been taking it alone.

"I just started this week," I told her. "But I used to ski."

"Boards are so much better."

"Yeah, I have to agree."

"I gotta laugh when I see those skiers with their sticks and poles, fumbling around to get it all in place. And all we gotta do is ride." She pointed to a skier who just wiped out below us, a mess of skis and poles all over the place.

"Man," she said. "Look at that garage sale down there."

I laughed as the guy got up and started retrieving his stuff.

"By the way, I'm Maggie," she said as we came to the top.

"I'm Kim," I said as I got my board straightened up to make what I hoped would be a graceful exit from the chair.

"Want to go down together?"

"Sure." I held on to the chairlift pole, balancing my weight to slide off the seat. "But I'll warn you that I'm still a beginner."

"No problem."

So we both got off, and she waited for me to make my way over to her and then adjust my bootstraps. Then she gave me a few tips, and I followed her lead and thankfully didn't wipe out until we were nearly halfway down. And even then it wasn't too bad. I managed to get back up without even making a full stop.

"Good job," she called out. "Just get back on and keep riding."

I rode with Maggie for the rest of the day, and Dad actually seemed relieved to spend the afternoon with Mom.

"You going to be here tomorrow?" she asked as we took our last ride before the lifts closed at four.

"Yeah, we don't leave until Sunday morning."

"Want to hang together tomorrow too?"

"Sure," I told her. And so we agreed to meet for breakfast at the lodge restaurant in the morning and get an early start.

"That's great," my dad said when I told him about our plans. "Maybe I can take your mom for a sleigh ride."

"She'd love that," I said. And I could tell he was relieved that I'd found a snowboarding buddy. Not that he wasn't enjoying the skiing; I really think he was. But I also think he felt bad about leaving Mom on her own so much of the time. Although, she seems fine and hasn't complained at all.

Still, I know that we're both feeling a little torn about her right now. On one hand, we all act like everything is just peachy, perfectly normal. But at the same time, it's like we're walking on eggshells too. Like we're all thinking the same thing—is this going to be the last time we'll be up here as a family? Is this our last Christmas all together? And even though we're all having a pretty good time, it's like there's this dark shadow hanging over us.

Five

Saturday, December 31

On our last day at the ski lodge I try to make the most of it, hitting the lifts as soon as they open. I don't see Maggie anywhere, but after a couple of solo runs, I spot my dad's red and black ski parka, and we take a few "kinder, gentler" runs (as he calls them) until it's nearly noon.

"Do you mind if I take your mother into town for a special New Year's Eve dinner this evening?" he asks me as we head to the snack bar for a lunch break. "Or you could come with us if you like, but you'll have to give up a couple hours of snowboarding."

"No way. I'd rather get in a full day. Especially since we're going home tomorrow morning." But I don't tell him, I suspect that he and Mom might enjoy a more romantic dinner with just the two of them.

He picks up a bowl of chili topped with cheese.

"Mom wants to have a little nap first. But we'll probably leave around two or three. Give her some time to look around town before the shops close."

"She'll love that."

"You sure you don't mind?"

"Not at all, Dad. I'll probably just get a quick dinner then crash."

"You don't plan to see in the New Year?" he teases.

I roll my eyes at him.

"I think I'll go have a little rest myself," he tells me as we finish up our lunches. "You already wore me out." He smiles now. "You're getting pretty good on that snowboard, Kim. You really like it?"

"I totally love it, Dad!" I'm tempted to tell him that I want to get a snowboard of my own now, but I realize how much money he's already spent on this trip, and I keep my mouth shut.

"Well, don't tear up the slope too much this afternoon. And remember, you can call me on my cell if you need anything tonight."

"Right. Like I want to interrupt your dinner. Don't worry, Dad. I'll be just fine. You guys have a great time and stay out as late as you like." I wink at him. "And happy New Year."

He laughs. "I'm sure that we'll probably both wear out long before midnight. And it's almost an hour drive back here, so I don't think we'll stay in town too late."

I finish off my soda then stand up. "Guess I'm off then." He stands, kisses me on the cheek, then reminds me as usual to "be careful" up there.

"Yeah, yeah. And tell Mom Happy New Year for me." I start gathering up all my stuff to head back outside. "And have fun too!"

He nods. "I'm sure we will."

"Hey, Kim," calls Maggie as I head for the main door to the lifts. "I was just looking for you. Ya ready to rock and roll?"

"Sure. Where ya been?"

"My parents insisted on all of us going out to breakfast together. Problem was my little brother didn't get up until around ten. I can't believe I missed the whole morning."

As we're going up in the blue chair, she tells me about a New Year's Eve party that she's been invited to. "Want to come?"

By now I know Maggie well enough to know that she's not a Christian, but I still really like her and enjoy her company, not to mention the free snowboarding lessons. And I've actually been trying to share my faith with her. Okay, I'm not very good at this yet. I mean, sometimes I barely know what I believe myself. But I feel this need to talk to her about my faith, and I'm hoping it's a God-thing. Anyway, I know she's been turned off by Christians in the past so I'm really trying not to be too pushy. Although I finally did tell her that I was a Christian yesterday.

"No way," she said. "You don't seem like that at all."

"What do you mean? Like what?"

"I mean you're not all pushy and arrogant and full of yourself."

I kind of laughed. "Is that what you think of Christians?"

"Well, there are these Christian girls at my school," she explained. "And all they want to do is to get everyone saved. Like they don't really care about you personally or what might be going on in your life, they just want you to come to their church and get saved like it's some kind of contest where they get a gold star or a notch on their belt or something. And I just don't get that."

So I told her a little about my own spiritual journey, how I studied Buddhism and some other Eastern religions. "I'd gone to church as a kid, but I just didn't buy into it. I wanted to try some other things and see if I could find something that really worked for me."

"That's cool," she said, actually impressed.

"Yeah, it was pretty interesting studying the various religions," I admitted. "And Buddhism seemed to make a lot of sense at first. But it didn't really have what I needed. And ultimately, it just made me feel worse about myself. Like I would never be able to really succeed at it, and I knew I'd never make a very good Buddhist."

"That's why I try to avoid religion altogether. It's like a lose-lose situation if you ask me." Then the lift reached the top and we took off down the hill. And it seemed the moment was gone. At least for yesterday.

But today I've been really praying that I'll be able to say something that will make a difference to her. But I so don't want to be like those girls at her school. I mean, I'll probably never see her again anyway, and it's not like I'm looking for a gold star. I just really care about her, and I've heard enough about her life and her family to know that she's not happy. In some ways she reminds me a lot of how I was before I committed my life to God. Kind of searching but in denial.

So I decide that's what I'll tell her (that she reminds me of me), but it seems that the conversation just never really gets to that place. Finally we're taking our last lift up, and I'm feeling kind of desperate to say something, but she's talking about snowboarding and telling me what kind of board I should get and which websites to look for it on, and suddenly it's time to get off and ride down the hill.

Naturally, I'm really into the ride and having a great time, and as a result I don't even see this kid on skis who's cutting through the trees, totally out of control and heading straight at me.

"Look out!" Maggie yells. But it's too late. He slams right into me and literally knocks the wind out of me. My board flips up, and I land on my back, knocking my head into the hard-packed snow with a brain-jarring whack, which makes me feel like I can see stars. The next thing I know, Maggie is standing over me, asking me if I'm okay and yelling at the kid who's making a getaway.

"Yeah," I gasp, still trying to catch my breath as I sit up and rub my head. "I think so."

"Just breathe slowly," she tells me, flopping down to sit beside me. "Try to relax and then see if anything hurts."

I sit there for a while and try to take a kind of inventory. My arms and legs seem fine, and I can breathe, so I think I'm pretty much okay. Just shaken.

"That really scared me," I finally admit as I continue to rub my head, which is throbbing now. I wonder if it's possible I've suffered brain damage, which actually seems pretty ridiculous, although I've noticed how a lot of skiers and boarders are wearing helmets these days. My dad even questioned me about it a couple of times.

"Me too," she says. "I thought you were a total goner. Stupid skiers! We should report that moron to the ski patrol."

"I think he was as shocked as I was when he hit me."

"Well, he didn't even apologize. Just took off like he knew he was going to be in big trouble."

I look at the sky, which is now a dusky blue. "Guess we better get down before it gets dark, huh?"

"You sure you're okay, Kim? I could go for the ski patrol, and they could carry you down."

"No thanks," I tell her as I check the straps on my board. "I saw those guys practicing this week, and it looks like it'd be scarier riding down in one of those stretcher sleds than going down on my own."

"Let's just take it easy, okay?" She stays close to me

as I carefully start to navigate down the slope.

My legs are a little shaky and my head still hurts, but I'm thankful nothing is broken or sprained. I would hate having to call my dad while he and Mom are out on their New Year's date.

Finally we're back at the lodge. "Everything still okay?" she asks me again.

I nod. "Yeah. Just my head aches a little." Then I smile at her. "Hey, thanks for helping me, Maggie. I don't know what I would've done on my own."

"No problem. I've got some Advil in my pack if you want a couple for your head."

"Thanks, that's probably a good idea." Then I tell her that my parents are gone for the evening and that I'm going to get a snack and call it a night.

"No way," she tells me. "You should hang with me for a while. Just to make sure you don't have a concussion or anything. Let's go get my pack and turn in your board, then maybe we can find something decent to eat."

As we're eating cheese pizza from the snack bar, I actually get a chance to tell her a little bit more about my faith. And to my surprise she seems to be listening. I explain about how I saw "The Passion of the Christ" movie and how it really got to me.

"It's still kind of hard to understand," I tell her. "But it's like God was really talking to me, not literally. I mean, I couldn't actually hear His voice, but I got this very real feeling, like I could sense something clicking deep inside of me, and somehow I knew it was real. Does that seem too weird?"

She kind of frowns then slowly nods. "I actually believe you." Then she looks at her watch. "But I better get back to our cabin or my mom will think I've broken my neck on the slope."

I stand up now, sorry that our conversation is ending. "It's been cool snowboarding with you, Maggie. I really appreciate—"

"Hey, it's not over yet," she says as she puts a strap of her pack over one shoulder. "You're coming to that party with me, aren't you?"

"Oh, I don't—"

"You said yourself that your parents are gone for the night. Come on, Kim. I don't want to go by myself. And the guys seem nice. Remember the group that rode down with us before that last ride?"

"But I'm not into—"

"Please, don't tell me you're going to turn into one of those goody-goody Christians who judge everyone and everything and are too holy to associate—"

"Okay," I say suddenly. "I'll come with you. Just to see what it's like. But I reserve the right to leave if I want to, okay?"

"Okay." She smiles now. "I'm going to clean up and have a rest. I'll call your room around seven, okay?"

"That's cool."

Now as I walk to my room, I'm wondering if it was the blow to the head or just plain stupidity, but somehow I've agreed to go to what I'm pretty sure will be a drinking party. Still, I can leave if I want. The party's going to be in a condo unit right here in the lodge, and I can simply walk back to our cabin if I need to. And who knows, I might even get a chance to really talk to Maggie again.

So, like Maggie, I clean up a little and take a nap, but I'm startled awake by the ringing of the phone.

"You ready?"

I groggily look at the clock to see it's already past seven. "Yeah, I guess so." Then I go into the bathroom and check myself out in the mirror. Okay, I do wonder why I should care about my appearance since I don't really know these kids. But even so, I take time to put on some lip gloss and mascara, and I even fuss with my hair before I hear Maggie knocking at the door.

As it turns out, I was right. It is a drinking party that Maggie's been invited to. But it seems that the kids are mostly college aged, and everyone is acting pretty normal and a lot more mature than the way I've seen high school kids acting at parties like this at home (not that I've been to many). So, I decide to just relax a little, although I go for soda instead of the beer that Maggie pops open.

"You seem older than sixteen," she tells me as we go and stand by the fireplace.

"I'm almost seventeen," I say. I know that Maggie's a senior, but I also know that she's not as much into school or academics as I am.

Soon a couple of guys come over and start talking to us. Well, mostly to Maggie since I seem to be somewhat dumbstruck.

"I'm going to tour Europe after I graduate," she's telling them. And they tell her about a trip they took last year.

"It was awesome," the tall guy says. "We hit all the major ski resorts."

"Zermatt, Innsbruck, Chamonix..." the other guy (I think his name is Tyler) starts rattling off words that sound like a foreign language to me. What in the world am I doing here?

"How long have you been snowboarding?" the tall guy asks, and I realize he's talking to me.

"I just started this week," I manage to say.

"But she's doing pretty good," Maggie adds.

"I used to ski," I admit.

"Hopefully you've given that up for good," says Tyler.

I sort of laugh and wonder how I can make a graceful exit without offending Maggie.

"Can we get you girls another drink?" asks the tall guy.

"Sure," says Maggie. "I'll have another Corona."

"How about you?"

"I'm fine," I say quickly.

"That's not very festive," says Tyler. "Haven't you heard that it's New Year's Eve and people are supposed to be celebrating?"

I just shrug. "I'm not much of a drinker."

"How about something to warm you up then?" he offers, surely noticing how I'm hovering close to the fire. "Like peppermint cocoa?"

"Sure," I say, relieved that he's not pushing alcohol. "That sounds great."

"See this isn't so bad," Maggie says after they leave. "You just need to loosen up a little."

"Well, I'm probably going to leave soon. Hope you don't mind."

She frowns and shakes her head. "I guess that's the thing that really bugs me about Christians."

"What?"

"That you're afraid to have fun."

"I'm not afraid to have fun. I just don't happen to think that drinking alcohol equals fun."

"So you think it's wrong?"

I consider this. I mean, my parents have an occasional glass of champagne like at weddings and such. I wouldn't be surprised if they were having a glass tonight. And seriously, I don't think that's wrong. But then I remember the advice I gave for the column this week. "Well, I think it's wrong when you're underage."

She rolls her eyes at me. "So I'm old enough to vote or go into the military or get married, but I'm not old enough to drink a beer?"

I shrug. "According to the law."

"What about in Europe?"

"What about it?"

"The law is different there."

I shrug again. "But we're not in Europe."

She grins. "We can pretend."

I have to laugh at that. And now the guys are back with her beer and my cocoa. But when I take the cocoa it smells a little funny. "What's in this?"

"Peppermint," says Tyler. "Like I told you."

"Is it alcohol?"

"It's just for flavoring," he says. "Try it."

For some reason, I take a sip, and to my surprise it tastes okay. I mean, I've tasted alcohol before, and I really don't like it. But this just tastes like cocoa and peppermint, and before I know it I've finished it off.

"I should probably go," I tell Maggie.

"But this is New Year's Eve," protests Tyler. "And it's early."

"Don't be a party pooper," teases the tall guy.

"How about another cocoa?" asks Tyler.

So the next thing I know, I'm having another peppermint cocoa. And after that, things get a little blurry, but somehow I realize that it's the cocoa, and I start to feel a little freaked. "I've gotta go," I tell Maggie.

"What's wrong?" she asks.

"I don't feel very good."

"Is it your head?" she asks with genuine concern. Then she tells the people who are standing around us about the wipeout I had today.

"She really smacked her head," she finally says.

I nod, rubbing my head for what I hope is a good effect. "I think I need to go."

"You shouldn't walk back alone," she says.

"I could walk her back," offers Tyler.

Now this kind of scares me. I mean, I hardly know this guy. He's in college, and he's given me drinks laced with—who knows what? "No thanks," I say quickly. "I'm fine on my own."

"No way," says Maggie. "You might pass out and freeze to death in the snow."

Somehow I manage to find my coat and the door, but to my dismay, Tyler is still at my side. "I'm really okay on my own."

"You never know," he says as he takes my arm.

Okay, my heart is pounding now, and I'm certain that he plans to mug, beat, or rape me out here. My legs are shaking as I walk down the path toward our cabin. The walk has been shoveled, but it's icy and slick. I almost fall down, but Tyler manages to keep me on my feet. Finally we're at my cabin. "Thanks," I quickly tell him, bracing myself for I'm not even sure what.

"No problem." He walks me up to the door. "Happy New Year." Then he turns and walks away.

I fumble around for my key and, unlocking the door, slip inside then lock it behind me, waiting in the darkness to be sure that he's not coming back. Finally I realize that he's long gone and I'm just being extremely paranoid—whether it's from the cocoa or the blow to my head or simply a guilt attack for having gone to a drinking party.

I go straight to bed, but before I go to sleep I tell God

that I'm sorry for being such a hypocrite, and I ask Him to forgive me and to help me do better in the upcoming new year.

Six

Sunday, January 1

"You're awfully quiet," Mom said as Dad drove us toward home today.

"Just tired," I told her. But what I was really feeling is guilt. Plain old ordinary guilt. I can't believe that, after I wrote about it in my column and even lectured Matthew about it last week, I actually went to a drinking party and even inadvertently consumed two drinks last night. I really do feel like a total hypocrite now. Oh, I know that God forgives me. But I'm having trouble forgiving myself.

Not only that, I'm thinking of all the things that could've happened or gone wrong last night. Like what if Tyler hadn't been such a nice guy? Or what if someone had put something even stronger in my drink? I mean, there I was with a bunch of complete strangers, all older than me, and I was drinking! It just boggles my mind, and I'm more ashamed of myself than I can admit—to anyone besides God, that is.

I cannot begin to imagine what Nat would say to me about this. And even Matthew, although I think he'd understand, but I'm sure I'd lose some respect in his eyes. I wonder what Maggie thinks of me. And here I thought I was going to share my faith with her. All I did was manage to look like a total idiot. Aghh!!!

After we get home, I try to distract myself by practicing violin, and though it works for a while, I am still feeling really guilty for making such a stupid decision last night. What is wrong with me? Okay, I realize that I'm human. I'm not perfect, and I'm expected to blow it occasionally. But it still really bugs me.

Finally I decide to respond to some letters for this week's column. Maybe I think it's like doing penance, or maybe it's the old Buddhist thinking coming back. But I hope that doing something "good" might help to alleviate this feeling of guilt that keeps gnawing at me. Naturally, the first letter I pick up has to do with alcohol. It figures!

Dear Jamie,

When I was fifteen, I started drinking at parties and stuff with my friends. I thought it was just to have fun and loosen up. But now I'm seventeen, and I think I might have a drinking problem. I don't just drink with friends anymore. I drink when I get up in the morning. I go home for lunch so I can drink some more, or I sneak vodka into school in my water bottle. My parents are beginning to suspect that I've been sneaking alcohol from their liquor cabinet (which is true), but I also have a friend who buys it for me. This year my grades have really slipped, and if I don't get it together, I might not graduate in spring. Do you think it's possible that I'm an alcoholic? What should I do?

Boozer Girl

Okay, this might require some research on my part. This is a serious question, and I don't want to sound glib or trite in my answer to her. So I go online to do some research on teen alcoholism. I'm somewhat shocked to learn that millions of teens are confirmed alcoholics, and millions more have "drinking problems that are out of control." I also learn a number of other disturbing things that I will include in my response to Boozer Girl.

Dear Boozer Girl,

Here's the good news—you are admitting you have a problem. *Yes, it's quite likely you are an alcoholic, but you are not alone. Millions of teens have the same problem. More than three million teens are currently seeking help for their addiction. Help can be found through twelve-step self-help support groups like AA or by getting advice and support from a health care professional.*

Here's the bad news—if you don't get help, your life is at serious risk. According to statistics, the three leading causes of teen deaths (automobile accidents, suicide, homicide) are almost always related to alcohol abuse. But even if you cheat death, you will probably suffer other problems like depression, anxiety, or a variety of other social disorders that can really ruin your entire life.

In other words, alcoholism is an extremely serious disease that you should get help for immediately. If you find you're unable to talk to your parents about your drinking problem, go to a school counselor, church counselor, or your own physician to find help. Be honest about how much and how often you drink, and make a plan with this person for a way to inform your parents. Chances are they will be as concerned as you are and want to help you find the help you need. But if they're not, you still need to get help ASAP. Don't put this off.

Just Jamie

Realizing that the letter was not only longer than usual but pretty heavy in content, I decided to run it by my dad. I printed it out, then found him in his office, working on his computer. His face seemed fairly concerned, so much so that I decided not to interrupt him.

"Oh?" he said as I was just turning to leave. "Kim, I didn't even see you there." He removed his glasses, rubbed the bridge of his nose, then sighed deeply. "What's up?"

I approached his desk. "I was about to ask you the same thing. You look kind of troubled, Dad. Something wrong at work?"

He shook his head and glanced back at his screen, then I bent over to see what he was looking at. It turned out to be one of the very same cancer sites I'd looked at recently.

"Oh." I sank onto the chair across from his desk. "I've read that one too."

"I don't know why I bother. It's mostly just depressing news."

"But you keep hoping you'll find something new and encouraging."

He nodded. "Yeah, some amazing medical breakthrough that will change everything."

"I've kind of decided to avoid researching it anymore," I admitted. "It just gets me too bummed."

He switched off his computer screen. "Maybe I should follow your lead." Then he looked at the paper in my hand. "What's that?"

"A letter for the column. I thought maybe you should read it first." I handed it to him and waited for him to skim over it.

"This sounds well done to me, Kim. I'm assuming your facts are correct."

I nodded. "Yeah, I checked it online. Pretty sad, huh?"

"It's too bad." He handed the paper back. "By the way, I think you're doing a really great job on the column. Charlie is very happy with the responses we've been getting."

"Cool." Now I considered confessing everything to

him, telling him about the irony of me answering a letter about teen alcoholism after I was a guest at a drinking party just last night. But he already has Mom and her problems weighing heavy on his mind right now. Why add to his stress?

"I really had a great time snowboarding last week," I finally said for lack of anything else. "Thanks again for taking us up there."

He kind of smiled. "I expect you're ready to trade in your skis for a snowboard now."

I laughed. "Anything wrong with that?"

He shook his head. "You're a working girl, Kim. Plus you have the Christmas money that Uncle Steve and Grandma Peterson sent. If you want to buy a snowboard, that's entirely up to you."

"Maybe I should look into a helmet too," I told him.

"Now, that sounds like good thinking to me."

I rubbed the back of my head. "I actually had a wipeout yesterday. It kind of shook me up, and I found myself wishing I'd taken your advice and rented a helmet."

"How about if I spring for the helmet. After all, your mind would be a terrible thing to waste, Kimmy."

I had to laugh at that. "Thanks, Dad; that'd be great. Maybe I can get it in time for the church snow trip."

And so it was that I never told him about my little drinking episode. I feel sort of bad, but at the same time, I don't think he really needs anything else to worry about right now. Even so, I still feel a little guilty—or maybe it's just hypocritical.

Tuesday, January 3

Matthew is quite impressed that I took up snowboarding. I think it's what helped to convince him to come to snow camp with our youth group next weekend. I haven't told him that I'm not bad for a beginner. I figure I'll let him make up his own mind about it when we get up to the snow.

"I wish I could get a snowboard before then," I tell Matthew during art.

"Why don't you?"

"Well, I looked online yesterday, and I'm not really sure what I want. Besides, it probably can't get here by Friday now."

"Why don't we go into the city to look around?" he suggests. "I know of a good shop, and they might even have some good deals since Christmas is over with."

"Seriously?"

"Yeah. It's worth a try."

So I call my mom and tell her about my plan, and she seems okay with it. "Just drive safely," she says like usual.

"Take care," I tell her then hang up. It occurs to me after hanging up that I never even asked how she was doing. I know she went to a doctor's appointment today, and I should've asked. But I also know that she doesn't really like to talk about it. Besides, I've been praying so hard that God will heal her. And I'm really believing that it can happen.

"You're going to the city with Matthew?" Natalie asks

me during lunch. She has a suspicious look, and I can tell she's not really comfortable with my relationship with Matthew. But I don't see what the big deal is. It's not like we're really dating anyway. We're mostly just good friends.

"Yeah," I tell her. "And if it makes you feel any better, he's decided to go on the snow trip with our youth group."

Her eyes light up now. "That's great, Kim. Maybe he'll get saved after all."

Somehow this comment kind of bugs me, and it reminds me of what Maggie said about the Christian girls at her school. "So, are you saying that you'd accept Matthew if he was saved?"

She kind of shrugs. "What do you mean?"

"I mean, it seems as if you don't like him very much, Nat."

"I worry about you dating a non-Christian, Kim. You know that."

"We're not really dating."

"Yeah, whatever."

"It just bugs me that you keep drawing this line between non-Christians and Christians. It seems like segregation or discrimination or something. Do you really think that's how Jesus wants us to treat people? I mean, think about it. When Jesus started ministering on earth, NO ONE was a Christian. And He hung out with everyone. In fact, according to what I read in my Bible, He was pretty down on the religious guys who acted like they were better than everyone else."

Nat looks slightly offended now. "Are you saying that I'm like that?"

"Not exactly...but sometimes you can come across that way."

"Well, my youth pastor is always reminding us that light and darkness don't mix. And he warns us against dating non-Christians."

"Matthew and I are NOT dating."

"Call it what you like, Kim. But you're getting more and more involved with him. I mean, you guys exchanged Christmas presents."

"I thought you were okay with that."

"I'm trying to be okay with it, Kim. For your sake. But I still worry about you. You're still kind of a baby Christian and—"

"A baby Christian?" Now this really irks me. "What's that supposed to mean?"

"It's from the Bible, Kim." Now, if you ask me, the tone of Nat's voice is sounding pretty condescending. "And it means that you haven't been walking with the Lord long, and you might get tripped up pretty easily, especially if you start dating a non-Christian."

I take in a deep breath and literally bite my tongue to keep from saying something I might regret.

"Don't get all offended," she says quickly. "I'm only telling you this because I love you, Kim. I don't want to see you get hurt. And I really don't want to see you falling away from the Lord."

"Sorry, I can't give you a ride home," I say in a flat voice.

"That's okay," she says lightly. "I'll ask Cesar for a lift."

Poor Cesar, I'm thinking as I wait for Matthew to meet me after school. I mean, Natalie still has this huge "secret" crush on him. And Cesar is still committed to not dating. And in all fairness, Nat is pretty good-looking. I wonder if it's tough for him to be around her when she's practically throwing herself at him. Okay, she's not throwing herself. Nat's got more class than that. Marissa's the one who throws herself at him.

"Hey, Kim," says Matthew. "Ready to roll?"

I smile at him and wonder why Nat insists on making such a big deal about him being a "non-Christian" and who came up with that word anyway? And I gotta ask myself, what would Jesus do?

I already know that Matthew went to Robert's New Year's Eve party but also that he got disgusted and left. And he actually admitted that he was tempted to stop by the skating rink and that he would've if I'd been there. But he felt uncomfortable showing up at a church party on his own.

"They would've made you feel welcome," I had assured him. "And Cesar would've been there..." But he wasn't convinced. At the time I was tempted to tell him about what I did on New Year's Eve, but somehow I just couldn't bring myself to admit to being such an idiot.

However, as I'm driving into the city, I decide that it's time to come clean with someone. Maybe it has to do with my conversation with Nat and feeling like I'm a bit of a hypocrite, but I decide to just spill the beans with Matthew.

"No way!" he practically yells after I finish my little tale.

I nod without looking at him. "And it's not like I'm proud of myself. In fact, I'm really feeling—"

"I cannot believe you did that, Kim, especially after the way you raked me over the coals just for considering going to Robert's party."

"Raked you over the coals?"

"Well, you were pretty adamant about me not going."

"I just didn't think it was a good idea. I don't think—"

"But it's okay for you to go out partying with a bunch of college kids who you don't even know. And then to drink—"

"I didn't know there was anything in the cocoa," I tell him again.

"Peppermint Schnapps," he says.

"Huh?"

"That's what they put in your drink. Some people call it a Peppermint Patty."

"Oh..."

Now he pats me on the shoulder. "It's okay, Kim. I'm not trying to get down on you. In fact, I think it's kind of cool that you stepped out of your little shell."

"My little shell?"

"You know, the little Christian protective shell that some—"

"I don't have a Christian protective shell!"

"Hey, don't get mad. You're not as bad as Natalie. She wears hers like it's a superman cloak that will protect her from everything."

"Do you really see it like that?"

"Kind of..."

"I'm surprised you'd want to go on the snow trip retreat then."

"Well, I'm hoping the boarding will be good. Besides, you're going." He playfully pokes me in the arm now, and I'm not sure how to respond. Between Matthew and Natalie, I'm feeling a little confused. "And Cesar's going too," he adds. "And I think he's an okay guy."

"Really?" For some reason this gives me hope.

"Oh, he's a little uptight when it comes to chicks. But you gotta respect him for sticking to his convictions. I'm sure it's not easy."

"So, have you lost respect for me?" I ask in a weak voice. "I mean, because of going to that party? Do you think I'm a hypocrite?"

"Not at all. I guess I think you're still trying to figure some things out, Kim. And I actually respect you because you're honest about it. You didn't have to tell me, you know."

"Yeah, I know."

"It's those Christians who act like they're all perfect that bug me. At least you're not like that."

"Thanks, I think..." Suddenly I'm remembering things that Maggie said to me, and I'm feeling pretty uncomfortable.

"Have you ever seen that movie 'Saved'?"

"I've heard of it, but I've never seen it."

"You should rent it sometime. Maybe invite Natalie over to watch it with you." Then he kind of laughs. "Just don't tell her the title, or she might flip out."

Before long we're downtown, and I'm looking for a place to park near the snowboard shop. I'm not sure why, but I feel a little better now that I told Matthew about blowing it. And it's not because he was okay with it as much as I felt I owed it to him, especially after being so down on him about the possibility of going to Robert's party. And I suppose, like they say, confession really is good for the soul.

We look at lots and lots of snowboards, and the sales guy is really pretty helpful and knowledgeable. But talk about an information overload. After a while I'm feeling pretty overwhelmed, plus most of the ones he's shown us are way out of my ballpark.

"It's not like I need the best board out there," I finally say. "I mean, I'm still just a beginner. The girl I hung with last week suggested I get a Lamar. Do you have any of those?"

He scratches his head. "As a matter of fact, I just got one returned. It was a Christmas present, but the girl's mom said 'no way.' Her daughter was like twelve, and the dad had gotten it, but the mom thought she was too young to take up snowboarding. Of course, we thought that was totally bogus. I mean, I know kids who aren't even school aged who tear up the slopes on their boards. Anyway, she brought back a Lamar Fascination, and it's all set for someone just about your size."

Okay, it's kind of insulting that he thinks I'm the size of a twelve-year-old, but then I can't really argue with him either since it's probably true. "Can I see the board?"

He goes into the back and emerges with a blue snowboard and a pair of boots. "These boots are pretty small. Women's size six," he says a bit tentatively, and I actually clap my hands.

"I wear a six!"

Within seconds I have on the boots, am clamped onto the snowboard which has some very cool graphics and great shades of blue, and am trying it out on this shag carpet-covered box they've designed specifically for this purpose. As far as I can tell it's perfect, but I don't want to let on. I sit back down to remove the boots and then look up at the salesman.

"I don't have a lot to spend on this," I say slowly. "I'm guessing it's going to be too much."

"Well, this board retails at about three hundred dollars."

I firmly shake my head. "No way," I say sadly. "I can't afford—"

"Wait a minute. I'm trying to make you a deal here. Because of the return and the fact that this pretty much needs to be sold as a package, we can give it to you for quite a bit less. Let me go talk to my boss."

So he leaves for a while, and Matthew assures me that they should give me a good deal. "They'd have a hard time finding anyone who fits that board package the way it's set up now. It's really in their best interest to make you happy and get rid of it while they can."

"Do you know that I actually prayed about this?" I suddenly tell him. "Just as we were walking into the store, I shot up this quick silent prayer that God would help me find the perfect snowboard, or else that I'd simply forget about the whole thing and just rent one during snow camp."

"Well, that Lamar looks about perfect for you."

After a couple of minutes, the manager comes back out with the sales guy and tells me I can take the entire package off their hands for a mere $150. I try not to act too surprised. But I do thank him—several times in fact. Then I ask the salesman to help me find a good helmet. "I promised my dad that I'd get one," I explain to him and Matthew.

"I can't believe it," I say as Matthew helps me carry the stuff to my Jeep. "It was like a real live miracle."

"I'm surprised to hear myself saying this, Kim, but I gotta agree with you there. That whole package would've been close to five hundred dollars at regular price. I mean, I know they give good deals, but that was a total steal!"

"God IS good!" I shout as I unlock the Jeep.

He laughs and carefully slides my new board into the back of my car. "Well, at least He's good to you, Kim."

Seven

Thursday, January 5

I'm so excited about the snow retreat! And here's the latest greatest news—Natalie is coming too! She was feeling bad during lunch yesterday. We were all sitting there talking about how cool it was going to be, and she was really wishing that her church would have a ski trip.

"I don't see why anyone would want to go to any kind of church camp," said Marissa. "I was forced to go to one once, and I swore that I'd never do that again."

"And you've been swearing ever since too," Jake added with a grin.

"Maybe it's time you tried it again, Marissa," said Chloe. "According to my brother, Josh, this one is supposed to be really good." But Marissa looked unconvinced.

"And you and Allie are both going too?" Nat said with a longing voice. She still acts a little bit like a groupie sometimes when it comes to Chloe's band.

"Yeah. It's the last fun thing we get to do before we go back on tour."

"Man, I wish I could go." Nat sighed.

"Why don't you just come along," suggested Cesar. "It's not like you have to belong to our church. Josh, our youth pastor, said we can invite anyone we want."

"And Matthew's coming," I reminded her.

"Yeah," said Matthew. "And I don't go to church anywhere."

Marissa dramatically rolled her eyes and stood up. "You guys make me wanna hurl." She looked directly at Matthew. "I don't know how you can stand it for a whole weekend."

Fortunately Matthew seemed to ignore her. But I must admit to being a little worried about how he'd react to being cooped up with a bunch of Christians for that long.

Nat told Cesar that she'd think about it, but when she and I were alone, she admitted to me that she couldn't afford it anyway. "Especially after Christmas," she said. "I'm pretty much broke, and Mom's in debt up to her eyeballs. You should've seen the stuff she got for us kids. She knew our dad wasn't going to do anything for anyone, so she maxed out her credit cards. It'll probably take her a whole year just to catch up."

"That's too bad," I told her, but by then it was time to go our separate ways. Then, seeing Cesar on my way into chemistry, I got an idea.

"Hey, Cesar," I said in a lowered voice. "Do you think Faith Fellowship ever offers scholarships for kids to go to things like snow camp?"

"You mean for Natalie?"

I nodded.

"I could talk to Josh."

"I might be able to contribute a little," I told him.

"I'll get back to you on it."

And as it turned out, they do have a "scholarship" fund. Cesar, Jake, and I all contributed to it, and an "unknown benefactor" covered the rest. At first Nat was a little embarrassed about being a "charity case," but then I reminded her that God is the one who should be credited for this. "You wouldn't want to push His gift away, would you?" So it's set—she's going!

My new snowboard is leaning up against the wall in my bedroom, and I'm just itching to get out there on it. But I must admit that I felt a little guilty when I realized that Nat doesn't even have a board. I considered loaning her my skis, but they'd be way too small. And she doesn't know how to ski or snowboard for that matter. But then I heard that a lot of the kids, including Cesar, are going to be tubing anyway. So my guess is she'll be okay with that. I just hope she's not going on this retreat in an attempt to hook up with Cesar. That would be so totally stupid.

Sometimes it does seem unfair that Nat's family is struggling so hard. Her mom trying to support three kids while the dad is God only knows where. He never sends them a penny. And then here I am an only child, and my parents, though not rich, are very generous to me. Not for the first time, I'm thinking that I need to learn to be more generous. I guess I should ask God to show me ways that I can do that.

In the meantime I want to get a couple of letters done for next week's column. The first one I read has to do with giving, and I think it might do me good to answer it.

Dear Jamie,

I just watched this TV show that had a special segment about all these kids in Africa and how their parents had died from AIDS so that now they're orphans and they're living in these really awful conditions with up to twenty kids per hut and how they struggle just to get clean water and enough food to survive and a lot of them are sick with AIDS too and it just seems so totally unfair that I feel guilty for having a nice house and food and clothes and stuff and I just wish there was some way I could help them but I don't know what to do and it's making me really depressed.

Guilty Guy

Wow, talk about your run-on sentences and total lack of punctuation. But this guy is actually making a pretty good point here. And so once again, I'm going to do some research on the Internet and see what I can come up with.

Dear Guilty Guy,

I know what you mean about feeling guilty about having so much when there are others with so little. In fact, your letter motivated me to do a little online research, and I actually discovered an organization that I have decided to partner with myself. It's the World Vision, and they have a fantastic track record for giving. But what really got me was that you get to sponsor a real child from anywhere in the world, and they send you the photo and updates and everything. So I decided to "adopt" a girl from Uganda—an AIDS orphan just like you wrote about. Her name is Sarai, and she's ten years old. And for only twenty-five dollars a month, she will have food, clothes, shelter, and schooling. What a deal! Anyway, this is their website—in case you or any other reader is interested in making a difference out there. http://www.wvi.org/wvi/home.htm Thanks so much for bringing this up!

Just Jamie

I checked with my dad first, just to make sure this is okay to do, plus I had to promise him twenty-five dollars (from my next paycheck) so he could use his credit card for my sponsorship of Sarai. I'm so excited about this. I printed out her photo from the website, but they'll send me a packet with more information later. Already, I'm wondering if I should sponsor more kids. And my parents are looking into it too. And who knows what Guilty Guy's letter might inspire others to do. This is so cool! The next letter I answer isn't quite as encouraging, but I felt like I couldn't ignore it either.

Dear Jamie,

I'm considering suicide. I know some people think that it's wrong to take your own life, but I don't see how I can go on living. Every day seems to be more painful than the last one. I just can't see any reason for me to continue. I don't even know why I'm writing this letter to you. I guess it's just my last pathetic cry for help.

Totally Hopeless

Dear Totally Hopeless,

First of all, I'm sorry that your life is so painful. I don't know what your circumstances are, but I do know your circumstance will probably improve—eventually. I think everyone goes through dark times when it seems hopeless. But those times don't last forever. On the other hand, suicide is forever. Death is final. You don't get a second chance. I believe that God put you on this planet for a reason, and it's not up to you to decide when it's time to exit. Why not ask God to help you—to give you a reason to live? And consider this, you think life is bad now, what if you killed yourself and discovered that you made a huge mistake—a mistake that could never be undone? How miserable would you be then? Talk to a counselor or youth pastor or trusted friend. Tell them how you feel and get help now.

Just Jamie

Both of the writers of these letters go onto my ever-growing prayer list, but I underline Totally Hopeless's name, and I spend about ten minutes really praying for her/him. I wish I could send my answer directly instead of waiting for the paper to run it on Tuesday. But hopefully God will watch over this person until then. And hopefully my response will encourage this person to reconsider. I was tempted to write about people who are struggling just to live—like AIDS orphans in Africa or moms with cancer in the U.S.—but I figured that might only dilute the message. Still, I'm not sure.

Eight

Sunday, January 8

The snow trip was totally awesome! I'm not even sure what the best part was. Our cabin counselor was Josh Miller's fiancée, Caitlin O'Conner, and she was really great. Talk about a role model—I seriously hope that I'll be just a little bit like her someday. I'd heard good things about her from Chloe, but for some reason I wasn't convinced.

For one thing, she's really pretty. Now I realize that it's not fair, but sometimes I don't take really good-looking people too seriously. That's pretty judgmental on my part, but it's just how I am.

Anyway, when I first met her, I kind of assumed that this attractive blue-eyed blond chick might be kind of an airhead. Don't ask me why. I mean, my best friend, Natalie, is a pretty blue-eyed blonde, and, well, to be totally honest, she can be a little fluffy sometimes. Even so, I totally love her (just in case you're reading this, Nat, which you better not be!!!). And there's actually more to Nat than meets the eye.

Likewise, I discovered that Caitlin has real depth to her too. For starters, she really loves God—like totally and wholeheartedly and would do anything for Him. And she also has a heart for children and is willing to be a foreign missionary. For years she's been involved with this mission in Mexico that runs an orphanage, and she told us she wouldn't mind spending her honeymoon there! She said since she and Josh had already planned to volunteer there this summer, it might be that's where they go after the wedding. Go figure.

And it's not like Caitlin doesn't know how to have a good time. I mean, she totally enjoys life, she's in love with her fiancé, and she really knows how to have fun. She was great at getting girls to open up during our cabin times. I guess I was one of the more quiet ones, since I still feel unsure about a lot of things.

And it hasn't helped my confidence knowing that Natalie thinks I'm a "baby" Christian. So I kind of like to just keep my mouth shut when people are discussing "spiritual" things. Partly because I HATE looking stupid, and partly because I learn more by just listening. Even so, I had a couple of good one-on-one chats with Caitlin.

"Chloe told me that you don't believe in dating," I said to her as we shared a chairlift on Saturday morning.

Caitlin laughed. "Word gets around, doesn't it?"

"Well, I think you've inspired Cesar. You know he doesn't date either."

"Josh told me about that. And I have to respect him for it. It's not easy for a guy to make a commitment like that."

"So you really think it's wrong to date then?"

She thought about this for a moment. "It's a totally individual thing, Kim. Something you have to figure out for yourself."

"So how did you figure it out?"

"Well, I dated for a while in high school. I mean, not much really...it wasn't like I was going out all the time or anything like that. But there came a time when God made it crystal clear to me that it was wrong. At the time I thought that meant dating was wrong for everyone, and I kind of went on this campaign to convince all my friends to give up dating too."

She threw back her head and laughed loudly. "Man, they'd get so mad at me sometimes. They called me Preacher Girl and even started running when they saw me coming. I was pretty pathetic really. I think I'd gotten it into my head that I sort of knew it all—I mean, when it came to God's will and spiritual things."

"That kind of reminds me of my best friend," I said without thinking.

"Natalie?"

I nodded but felt embarrassed that I'd admitted as much.

Caitlin smiled. "I think Natalie has a good heart, Kim,

but like the rest of us, she might have some growing up to do too. In fact, she kind of reminds me of how I was at her age."

I thought that was a pretty nice compliment for Natalie but didn't say as much.

"It's taken time, and I still don't have it down, but I've learned that convictions have to come from God, Kim. If we create our own convictions, we usually fall into the trap of thinking we're performing for God—like we can make up all these rules and jump through these hoops, and somehow it makes God happy. But it just doesn't work that way."

I consider this, but to be honest I don't totally get it. I mean, I know God wants us to obey Him and to do what's right. I'm just not always sure what's right. "So, you're saying it's okay to date unless God tells you not to?"

"Something like that. But you have to be paying attention too. Some people assume that just because they don't audibly hear God telling them something that He's not. But sometimes He's sending us all kinds of signals and messages, but we're just not paying attention. You know what I mean?"

"Sort of."

We talked a while longer then somehow got onto the subject of her wedding, and to my surprise she asked me about playing violin for their ceremony.

"Chloe's the one who told me you were really good," she said. "But I'll totally understand if you're not interested."

"Not interested?" I echoed with slight disbelief. "Of course, I'm interested. Do you want me to audition?"

"Judging by what Chloe and Allie say, I don't think it's necessary. But how do you feel about 'Ave Maria'?"

"I think it's beautiful."

"And you know it?"

"Sure." I had to smile now since not only do I know it, but I recently learned it so I could play it for my mom during Christmas this year. "And really," I told Caitlin, "I'd love to play it for you and Josh." Well, I couldn't believe how excited she was about this.

"It's so amazing, Kim," she told me as we reached the crest of the hill. "Watching the way God is working to bring the wedding details together already. It's like I hardly have to do anything. Everything just seems to be falling into place. But I truly believe it's because Josh and I are doing this according to God's timing. That's really important."

I'm not sure that I'll ever have it as together as Caitlin O'Conner, but like I said, she's a pretty good role model for me to imitate. Although she tried to make it very clear to the girls in her cabin that she was just as human as the rest of us. And while I'm sure that's true, you can't miss the way girls like Chloe and Allie and the rest totally admire her.

Even Natalie was pretty impressed. "If I wasn't so involved in my own church, I'd consider switching over," she told me as we rode home today.

But it wasn't just Caitlin who made the weekend

special. Josh's messages were powerful too. He gave us all a New Year's challenge to allow God to become bigger in our lives. Even Matthew seemed to think about this during last night's meeting, although he never really said anything.

Now here's the funny thing. I thought Matthew was going on this trip to mostly spend time with me, and while we did ride a fair amount together, he spent a lot of his free time with Cesar and the other guys. And I actually felt slightly offended by this. Okay, I'm only human and a "baby" Christian at that. But I guess I'd expected Matthew to be a little more interested in me.

However, he was impressed with my snowboarding skill. And that was worth a lot! "I can't believe you only just started, Kim," he said after we completed a fairly challenging run (at least for me—although I tried to hide it). "You're doing really great."

"That's probably because I'm so short," I said. "Someone told me that short people have the advantage to maneuver more easily since we're so low to the ground. But then your weight gives you the advantage to go faster."

He laughed. "Sounds like you're making this into a science."

"Well, there is a science to everything," I said as we got onto the lift again.

"So, you're saying if we race this next run, I'll win?"

"Duh."

And so once we reached the top, Matthew

challenged me to a race. For some stupid reason I agreed, and that's the last I saw of him for quite some time since he rode the next few runs with Josh, Caitlin's brother Benjamin O'Conner, and some of the other youth group guys.

Okay, I should've been glad he was comfortable with these Christian dudes, but I felt a little left out too. Although it was fun hanging with Chloe and Allie. Those girls are a hoot and a half. Chloe's a really good rider, and Allie's a really good sport. It was Allie's first time, and she spent most of it floundering around in the snow while we tried to coach her. Finally she gave up and joined the tubers, and Chloe and I did a few more runs together.

Then this morning things with Matthew seemed to change. We knew we only had a half day to snowboard, and I was determined to make the most of it. As it turned out, Matthew was too. So we pretty much spent the entire morning together. And during our last run, Matthew thanked me for inviting him to come on the retreat.

"Josh has given me some interesting things to think about, you know," he told me as we paused midway on the slope to enjoy the view. "But it's not like I'm going to become a Christian anytime soon."

"That's okay," I said as I defogged my goggles.

Then to my surprise he put his arms around me and pulled me close. "I really do like you, Kim." He hugged me tightly.

I hugged him back. "I really like you too."

"Even if I'm not saved?" He looked down into my face now.

I smiled. "Even if you're not saved."

Then he kissed me. Just once, but it was very sweet. "Was that okay?" he asked as he stepped away.

I grinned as I adjusted my goggles and put my helmet back on. "Hey, it was better than okay," I yelled as I took off down the hill ahead of him. I felt like I was flying as I rode down. But I wasn't surprised to see him whizzing past me, easily beating me to the bottom of the hill. At least I didn't fall down.

So all in all, it was a fantastic trip. And when I got home, I went on and on about it to my parents. And they seemed pleased that I'd had such a good time. But then after I came up here to go to bed, it occurred to me (again) that I'd forgotten to ask about how my mom was feeling. But then maybe that's okay, maybe she'd rather not be reminded. Besides, we're all still praying for her. We even prayed for her in my cabin during the retreat, and everyone there agreed to keep praying for her until she is totally healed.

Saturday, January 14

I went out with Matthew tonight. I thought I'd talked him into going to youth group with me, but then he switched gears by suggesting we take in a recently released movie instead. And since it was a flick I'd been wanting to see, it wasn't too difficult for him to tempt me. Even so, I did feel a little guilty for skipping out on youth group tonight.

Okay, I guess I can officially say that Matthew and I really are dating now. At least that's what Nat calls it.

"Don't give me that 'we're just friends' bit," she told me on Friday. "I saw you guys kissing after school yesterday."

"Kissing? It was nothing more than a little good-bye peck."

"Call it what you like. It looked like kissing to me."

"So, what's the big deal? Everyone does it, Nat." I didn't mention that I see couples, on a daily basis, who not only kiss but look like they're going for the whole tamale if you ask me.

"The big deal is he's not saved."

"So it would be okay to kiss him if he was saved?" I asked.

"Well, it changes things," she told me, as if she was the self-proclaimed expert.

"Okay, you're right. He's not saved yet. But he's taking me to youth group tomorrow night. And you never know what God might be doing."

That seemed to pacify her. "Does that mean you're not going to youth group with Cesar?" Her eyes got that hungry look again, like she still thinks she might have a chance with Cesar.

"What difference does it make, Nat? You know where he stands. Why don't you give the poor boy a break? Nothing's changed about him and dating." I didn't remind her of how unsuccessful her advances during snow camp turned out to be. Cesar was like a rock wall—unmovable when it came to her attempts to soften him up. I also didn't ask her why she thinks it's okay to keep pestering Cesar when he's made his position perfectly clear, but it's wrong for me to date Matthew. Because in my opinion what she's doing is worse than what I'm doing. But what do I know since I'm a "baby" Christian.

"It's just so unfair," she said as we got into my Jeep.

As I turned the key in the ignition, I was trying to think of a way to change the subject. "So, Nat, are you saying it's okay for me to be with Matthew if we go to youth group?" I asked like I needed her permission. Yeah, sure.

"I guess that's okay."

I had to laugh. "Well, good. Thanks for your blessing."

"It wasn't a blessing."

"Yeah, whatever."

"I just don't want Matthew to drag you down, Kim."

"Maybe I'm dragging him down, Nat. Did you ever think of that?"

"Just remember you need to keep God as number one in your life. Don't let Matthew take over."

"He's not taking over," I assured her as I pulled out of the parking lot. "God is still number one."

She nodded. "Well, that's a relief."

But I must admit (at least to myself, not Nat) that I really do like Matthew a lot. He's so easy to be with and we really understand each other. Well, other than the God thing, I guess. But even so, I totally understand where he's at right now, since I was in almost the same place not all that long ago. And I really do believe that he will change, and who knows, maybe I'm supposed to be a part of that change. And honestly, I don't see anything wrong with going out with him. Or kissing. But these thoughts I must keep to myself. Nat would NOT understand.

And that's probably the reason I went online to chat with her tonight. Trying to make her understand how I feel. For one thing, I knew she'd find out that I skipped out on youth group, so I figured I better just lay my cards on the table and tell her.

Naturally, she thought that was terrible and that Matthew was already influencing me away from God, and the next thing you know I'll be a perfect heathen or maybe even a Buddhist again. So, I assured her that was not the case—at least I tried to assure her. And then I told her that I thought Matthew was actually getting closer to coming to God and that perhaps I was part of the equation. Of course, she was pretty skeptical. But she did seem somewhat appeased. Then I invited her to watch a movie with me tomorrow. I didn't tell her which one, but after church I plan to stop by the video store and rent "Saved." I don't see that it can do any harm.

Sunday, January 15

Natalie didn't much care for my selection of movies tonight. In fact, she almost took it as a personal attack on her beliefs. Now, I hadn't seen "Saved" before and was only going on Matthew's recommendation, but I must admit there were some things I liked about it. In some ways it reminded me of the movie "Mean Girls," only the mean girls in this movie were the "Christians."

Now, not all Christians are like that. In fact, I know quite a few who are very cool. And I'm guessing the negative ones are definitely a minority. Just the same, I sure don't want to be like that, but it does make you think...

"That is so stereotypical," Natalie said with disgust as we watched the movie. "Christian bashing from Hollywood. Wow, what a surprise! You know the only religious group that it's always open season on is Christians. If someone made a movie like this about Muslims or Jews, well, watch out! The ACLU would be called in, and the filmmakers would be accused of discrimination or maybe something even worse. But it's perfectly fine to make a movie like this about Christians."

I wanted to tell her to just watch the stupid movie, but I realized I was already in over my head. As it turned out, I missed enough of the movie that I may need to watch it again.

"And guess who made this movie, Kim? Probably some Hollywood atheist who totally hates Christians. It's just so unfair."

"I don't personally know who made the movie," I told her in a flat voice.

"Well, it's all wrong. They're making us look bad."

"We make us look bad," I said, perhaps a bit impatiently. Then she got really quiet, and I knew she was mad. I suggested turning the DVD off, but she wouldn't hear of it.

"We might as well finish it," she snapped at me. But I could tell that she'd already turned it off in her head.

When the movie ended, I turned off the TV and looked at Natalie. Her face was blank, but I could tell she was still smoldering.

"Sorry you didn't like it," I said.

She rolled her eyes. "Well, I suppose there were a couple of good parts, like it figures that Mary got pregnant—she should've known better than to mess around. But even so I get so tired of Christian bashing in general."

"Who bashes Christians?" I asked as I popped out the DVD.

"Everyone. I mean, everyone who's not saved—I mean, who isn't a Christian."

So I had to wonder if this movie was giving her second thoughts on her Christian vocabulary or perhaps just the word "saved." And while that wasn't my intent, I don't think it hurts to consider how we might seem to others in words as well as in actions.

"But don't you think that Christians can come across as, well, kind of superior know-it-alls sometimes?"

She seemed to consider this. "Maybe, I'm sure that some people do. But not all of us."

"I just think Jesus would want us to be more approachable," I told her. "I think He'd want us to be the kind of people that non-Christians would want to get to know better."

"That's what I think too."

"But do you think that Hilary Faye was approachable?" I asked.

"No, but she's just a ridiculous character, and that was all part of the Hollywood thing. They wanted to make her look really bad as a put-down to Christians in general."

Well, I wanted to point out that there were other Christians in the movie too, but I just let it go. No sense in getting into a big fight over it. So that's when we decided to go in the kitchen and make cookies and pig out, and I tried to forget all about the movie.

But now I'm thinking about it again. And I think maybe I will watch it once more, by myself this time. But first I need to do some letters for next week's column.

Dear Jamie,

Our dog just died. He was seventeen years old, and I'd been around him my whole life. And now he's just gone. What I want to know is, do you think dogs go to heaven? Do you think it's possible that I'll see him again?

Missing My Mutt

Dear MMM,

Okay, I'm no expert on this, but I'm wondering why God would create something as cool as a dog, allow him to be your friend and part of your family, and then–poof–that's it, he's gone? I think a loving God would have a place for animals in heaven. Because frankly, I don't think it would really be heaven without them. I hope I'm not wrong. In the meantime, I guess you can be thankful that you got to enjoy your dog for all those years.

Just Jamie

I almost added "because I had a dog once, and he got hit by a car when he was only three years old, and I still miss him sometimes." But that would be a giveaway since Nat knows all about Rumple (short for Rumplestiltskin), so I realized I better not mention it.

Nine

Tuesday, January 31

Man, I can't believe it's almost February, and I haven't written in my diary for almost two weeks. Not that there's been much to write about. Mostly the same old same old. School, homework, church stuff, my column, and Matthew. Nat is absolutely certain that I'm seeing too much of Matthew. But I think it's only because she's jealous. I think she's wishing she had a boyfriend too. So much so that I think she's finally going to give up on Cesar. Not that her efforts were accomplishing much.

"I'm praying that God will give me a Christian boyfriend before Valentine's Day," she announced after school today. Okay, I couldn't help myself—I had to laugh. And naturally, that just irritated her.

"Sorry," I said when her eyes narrowed, like I was about to get another lecture on why I should not be going out with Matthew the non-Christian. "Uh, do you have anyone in mind, specifically?" I said quickly, pretending to take her seriously, even though I think it's slightly ridiculous to pray to God for a boyfriend. I mean, God must have more important things to do.

"Well, there's that new guy from Minneapolis," she said thoughtfully. "The one Cesar introduced us to at lunch."

"Garth?"

"Yeah. Garth Edmonds."

"He seemed nice." Actually I was thinking he didn't really seem like Nat's type—not that I know what that is. But Garth was pretty reserved and quiet. Of course, he's still new here, and it must be tough.

"I was just about to invite him to my church," she said as I turned down our street.

"But Cesar beat you to the punch."

"Yeah. That Cesar—always messing me up."

I laughed. "I'm sure he didn't mean to. Besides, you can still invite Garth to your church, Nat."

"Yeah, but after he goes to yours...well, you know. He'll probably like Faith Fellowship better."

"You could go there too," I said, not for the first time. "I don't mean all the time, Nat. I know your mom likes for you guys to go together and stuff. But you could come to youth group, you know."

"Yeah. I've been thinking about it since the snow trip."

"So, any other prospects?" I asked as I pulled in front of her house.

"You mean for a boyfriend?"

"Isn't that what we were talking about?"

Now she turned to me and got a slightly mysterious look on her face. "Actually, I do have someone else in mind. I heard that he's not going with anyone right now. And I know he's a Christian."

"Do I know him?"

"Uh-huh."

"And he goes to our school?"

She nodded, and I tried to go over the available Christian guys who might interest Nat, but I was coming up blank. It couldn't be Jake, although he flirts with her enough. "I give," I finally said.

"Benjamin O'Conner," she proclaimed proudly.

I frowned. "But I thought he was going with Torrey Barnes."

"I heard they broke up."

"Since when?" Now I was thinking I'd seen that couple together last week. And I'm certain that Torrey was at youth group with him last Saturday night (when I actually talked Matthew into coming). But I knew better than to mention this. I could tell by Nat's expression that she was feeling hopeful.

"Since today."

"Today?" I studied my friend carefully, thinking, don't you want to at least wait until the body gets cold? But thankfully, I don't say this.

"Yeah. I heard it from Cortney Stein in the bathroom."

"Well, Cortney and Torrey are pretty good friends," I admitted. "I guess it could be true."

"Of course, it's true."

"So..."

"So, we'll just see what happens." Natalie opened the car door with a big grin. "After all, I AM praying."

I nodded and forced what I hoped was an encouraging smile. "Keep me posted."

She laughed. "Count on it."

Natalie and Benjamin, I'm thinking as I sit at my computer to respond to a couple of letters for this week's column. I guess there have been stranger couples. Okay, now I'm wondering, why don't I think this will work?

I mean, Natalie is a great person; she's kind and caring and a strong Christian. And really, so is Benjamin. And Natalie is a pretty good student, nothing outstanding, but consistent. And well, so is Benjamin. And Nat is really good looking (at least I think she is, although she can get down on herself at times). And Benjamin is very good looking too. In fact, they're both tall and have similar coloring with the blue-eyed blonde thing going on. So maybe they'd even make a good couple. Who knows?

Okay, I guess the truth of the matter is that Benjamin is kind of a jock. Oh, he's a nice enough jock and not the least bit stuck-up. But he's really pretty thick with the—how do I put this?—"popular" crowd.

Not that Nat and I are so unpopular, really, but we're just sort of outsiders when it comes to a certain group. A certain group that Benjamin is totally comfortable in. And while Benjamin never puts others down (not that I've seen anyway), he does continue to be part of the crowd that kind of runs everything at school. Some of them are Christians (like his ex-girlfriend Torrey), and some like Courtney are not. But this doesn't seem to bother Benjamin, and the truth is, that's something I admire about him. It's like he's not afraid to mix it up.

Enough obsessing over Natalie's life. I open some new letters for the column and finally settle on two letters that seem to pertain to my thoughts about Natalie.

Dear Jamie,

My best friend (make that ex-best friend) has kind of ditched me for a new set of friends. We'd been best friends since about fifth grade, and we promised that we'd always be friends. But then she started hanging with these popular kids, and the next thing I know she's acting as if she doesn't even know me. It hurts so bad to be treated like this that I'd like to just tell her off BIG-time. But at the same time, I still want to be her friend too. I want things to be like they used to be and I'm really lonely now. What should I do?

All Alone

Dear All Alone,

It's got to hurt a lot to lose a good friend like that. But if you guys have been friends for as long as you say, there might be a chance that you can be friends again someday. But you might need to be patient in the meantime. If I were you, I wouldn't pressure my old friend (or tell her off) because this might make her want to have nothing to do with you forever. But I would try to make some new friends (or at least one), and I would try to move on with my life. And who knows, your old friend might eventually get tired of her new friends and come back looking for you. Hang in there.

Just Jamie

Dear Jamie,

My best friend broke up with her boyfriend last week. And her boyfriend and I have always gotten along pretty good—as friends, you know? Like I never put the move on him or anything, but we have fun joking around. The thing is I really do like him, and my question is, how long should I wait before I say anything to him? I'm afraid if I wait too long they could get back together.

Ready and Waiting

Dear Ready,

I see a serious problem here. You say this is your "best friend" and you're ready to make the move on her ex? Something isn't right. I think you're seriously risking your friendship if you try to hook up with her ex just one week after they broke up. Read All Alone's letter (above) if you need to see what it feels like to lose your best friend…because that's what I think will happen if you follow through with this crazy scheme. Maybe in time (like a couple months at least) when you're certain they're not getting back together and when you've discussed this with your best friend, maybe then it would be okay. But if you care about your best friend, you better learn to practice some patience.

Just Jamie

Man, I'm thinking a friend like that could make you seriously rethink your enemies. And although Nat and Torrey aren't exactly good friends (more like acquaintances), it still seems tacky for Nat to make any sudden moves on Benjamin right now. Not that I think she's planning anything. I mean, Nat has more class than that. At least I hope so.

Saturday, February 4

Yesterday afternoon, Matthew left town to go snowboarding with his dad and will be gone for the whole weekend. And while I'm glad for him since he doesn't see his dad that much, I'm feeling a little lonely too. And that seems kind of pathetic since it's only been a couple of days. I hadn't realized how attached I've gotten to him. One thing, there is no way I would confess this bit of info to Natalie. In fact, I'm feeling a little irked at my best friend tonight.

She called me this morning, saying that she'd

decided to come to our youth group tonight and asking if it was okay for her to catch a ride with me. That was fine since I was planning on going solo anyway—something I'm not really used to but was willing to try. However, I had this sneaking suspicion that her sudden decision to come with me to youth group had as much to do with Benjamin as anything else. But I did not mention this to Nat.

So we get to youth group, and Nat immediately zones in on Benjamin. Oh, not so as anyone would notice (besides me, that is), but I can see her making a very subtle but definite effort to get over to where Benjamin is talking to some of the guys over by the snack table.

By the way, Torrey is nowhere to be seen, and I know by now it's a fact that these two have broken up. I don't know the details, but I do know it's true. Even so, it's been less than a week, and in my opinion, too soon for anyone, including Nat, to move in on Benjamin.

I watch as Nat fills a cup with ice and Diet Sprite (which she never drinks) then moves over to where several big bowls of chips are positioned on the table right behind where the guys are standing and talking. Now I know that Nat doesn't like chips because she says they're "nothing but fat," but she goes ahead and takes a small handful, pausing there for a moment to, I'm sure in retrospect, consider her next move.

Then to my total shock, she takes a big step backward, straight into Benjamin who turns around just in time to "accidentally" bump into her drink cup with his elbow and slop it onto the same sweater that her mom probably went into debt for during Christmas.

"Oh!" Nat says with wide blue eyes, like she is so surprised, and I'm thinking, "No way, Nat. This is way too obvious." But she continues her little charade, trying to brush the wet spot from her chest with the back of her hand.

"Sorry," Benjamin says as he runs to the table for a wad of napkins.

"No, that's okay," she says quickly as he hands her the napkins. "It was totally my fault. I'm so clumsy."

He stands there with his hands hanging helplessly down his sides as he watches her blotting the soggy spot on her pale blue angora sweater. "Man, I hope that's not ruined."

"No, no." She looks at him with those big blue eyes again. "It's okay. And it's really my fault. I'm the one who ran into you. I should've looked before I backed up." Now she gets this helpless kind of look on her face. "I feel so out of place here." Then she looks around like a deer caught in the headlights that's about to run. "I probably shouldn't have come here at all—"

"No," Benjamin says, falling right into her clever trap. "It's great you came. I mean, I've never seen you here before." He kind of laughs. "And dousing with soda isn't the ritual welcome for newcomers. Really, I'm so sorry—uh...I guess I don't know your name."

"Natalie," she says quietly, like she's suddenly feeling self-conscious now.

"Yeah, I remember that. Didn't I have economics with you last term?"

She nods with an expression that still looks somewhat unsure, like she doesn't quite remember who he is. Give me a break. "I think so."

He sticks out his hand. "I'm Ben O'Conner."

She shakes his hand. "Nice to officially meet you, Ben. I mean, I'm sure I've heard your name or seen you on the football field, but I don't think we've had an actual conversation before."

"Weren't you at the snow retreat last month?" he asks suddenly.

"Yeah. I came with my friend Kim Peterson." She turns and waves at me now. Is this her signal for me to join them? I wonder what role I'm supposed to play.

"Hey, Kim," Ben says as I walk up. "I didn't even see you over there. How's it going?"

I just shrug, feeling embarrassed for my best friend. "Okay, I guess. I see you met Natalie."

Ben nods. "It seems like we should've met before...but hey, better late than never, right?"

She smiles brightly. I mean, like her whole face is lighting up as if she's won the lottery. "Yeah, better late than never."

"And I hope you like this nutty group of kids," he says. "The leader over there is going to be my brother-in-law before long."

"Oh, yeah," Natalie says with what I know is fake realization. "Caitlin is your sister! Oh, I get it now. She is such a sweet person. I got to know her at the ski retreat. She is amazing."

"She's okay." Then he laughs. "Okay, she's better than just okay. For a sister, she's pretty cool."

We talk for a while longer, then the music starts and it's time to sit down. "Wanna sit with me?" Ben asks, I think just to be polite since we're still all standing together.

"Sure." Nat smiles like this idea is a complete surprise to her. So we go to sit down, and not to my surprise, Nat sits right next to Ben. I don't know why this bugs me so much. Maybe I'm just missing Matthew, or maybe I'm having PMS, but I feel like smacking my best friend across the side of the head. Talk about Christian love!

During the small group time, when we break into a group of three, Nat even asks him (and me too, of course) to pray for her since she's been "feeling a little out of things at her home church and doesn't know what to do about it."

"My mom's had a really hard year," she tells us (which is totally true), "and I guess she kind of needs me for moral support right now." And then she goes ahead and tells about her younger brother and sister and how much they miss their dad.

This surprises me a little, since sometimes Nat tries to pretend (around people besides me) that her life is totally together and cool. For some reason she's being really open tonight. Unfortunately, I think the reason might be Ben. But this confuses me. Like does she think she might win this guy through pity?

By the end of the evening, Nat and Ben are like old buddies. Ben is taking the role of helper and counselor, and Nat is proving herself adept at coming across as fairly needy and helpless. What is wrong with this picture?

"I'll be praying for your family," Ben assures Nat as we get ready to leave. "Let me know how it's going, okay?"

She nods and smiles. "Sure, if you really want to know."

He gets a very genuine expression now, and I know he's sincere. "I really do." Then he turns and looks at me. "And I'm still praying for your mom, Kim."

"Thanks, I appreciate it."

"See you guys around," he says.

I can tell that Nat would've liked to have stayed longer, but I have already had more than enough. It's all I can do not to scold her as we walk toward my Jeep. Finally we're inside, and I let out an exasperated sigh.

"What's up with you?" she asks innocently.

I turn and look at her in the dim church parking lot lights. "Are you kidding?"

She frowns. "What's wrong?"

"That whole poor little me act. I could've sworn you had a script in your back pocket."

"Kim!" Now she looks hurt.

"Nat!" I toss back at her.

"It's not like I lied," she says without looking directly at me.

"How about playacting?" I challenge.

"I didn't—"

"What do you call it, Nat?"

She shrugs. "Okay, I guess it was a little dramatic. But you know there's a little actress in me." Then she laughs.

"Try out for the next play," I suggest as I start the engine.

"Oh, Kim, don't be so down on me. I had to come up with a way to get his attention. What's it hurt if I spill a little diet soda on my sweater? It's my sweater."

This makes me laugh. "I knew something was up when you went for the Diet Sprite," I say between giggles. "You hate diet soda, and I've never seen you drink Sprite."

"I thought it would be the most stain free." She suppresses her own laughter.

Soon we are both laughing and playing back the whole evening.

"Oh, Ben," I say in a bad imitation of Natalie then break into song. "I'm a poor little lamb who has lost my way, blah, blah, blah."

"It wasn't that bad."

But the truth is, <u>it was that bad</u>. At least from my perspective. To me it was insincere and disingenuous, and I'm very embarrassed for my best friend. To Nat, I'm sure it was merely strategic, a way for her to get Ben's attention and sympathy. Will it work for her? I don't really think so, but only time will tell.

Ten

Friday, February 10

Go figure! Nat's harebrained scheme seems to have worked after all. Or maybe it's like she keeps telling me—maybe it's just God answering her prayer. Whatever the case, Ben asked her to go to the basketball game with him tonight, and she is flying high. I'm happy for her but still concerned about her tactics.

"See," she told me during lunch, right after Ben popped the question. "God was listening to my prayers."

"Just because Ben asked you out doesn't mean he's your new boyfriend."

"It's a beginning," she said. "The Bible says 'do not despise these small beginnings,' Kim."

"I'm not despising anything, Nat. Just trying to keep your feet on the ground."

"I don't want my feet on the ground," she said happily.

Now I really should be relieved that Nat's going to the game with Ben, since this means we won't be a threesome again with her tagging along with Matthew and me. That's been the case at the last couple home basketball games. "Do you want to sit together at the game?" I asked her.

"You and Matthew?" Her brow kind of creased as she considered this. "Do Matthew and Ben get along?"

I shrugged. "I don't think they know each other that well. Although Matthew did some snowboarding with Ben at the snow retreat."

"Well, I can mention it to Ben and then just see how it goes."

I nodded. But somehow I didn't think that Nat wanted Matthew and me to join them. Maybe it was because it's her first date with him. Or maybe it was because Matthew's "not saved." I'm not sure. But I told myself that I didn't really care. Not that I don't like Ben. I do.

So Matthew and I get to the game after it's already started, and the gym is totally packed out. We walk past the front row, and I spy Nat and Ben sitting in the midst of his friends. And I have to admit that Nat looks especially cute tonight and has on what I'm sure must be a new top. And for a moment, when Nat waves at me, I'm thinking maybe they can squeeze together and make a little bit of room so Matthew and I can join them. But it turns out it was only a wave, not an invitation to join them.

So Matthew and I climb up the bleachers until we finally find a spot in the nosebleed section. The air is hot and smells like dirty gym socks, and someone has spilled a soda on the bench so it's nice and sticky right where I'm going to sit. I don't want to sound like a whiner, so I go ahead and sit down, getting my jeans nice and sticky too.

I can tell that neither of us are really enjoying the game, and I'm sure not enjoying sticking to the bleacher. So we both decide to split at halftime.

"Want to get some coffee?" he asks as we walk through the icy parking lot to where he parked his pickup, about a mile away it seems.

"Sure," I tell him, relieved at the prospect of getting warm again. "Hopefully my jeans won't adhere themselves to a chair."

He laughs. "You should've told me about the sticky bench, Kim. I would've sat there."

"It's okay. These jeans are due for a wash anyway." But as I say this, I experience this unexpected rush of guilt. I think about Mom and how she does all the laundry in our house. How I take it for granted and just pile my clothes into the hamper, knowing that they will "miraculously" reappear all clean and pressed and smelling nice.

"You don't know how good you have it," Nat is always telling me. "I've been doing my own laundry since I was twelve."

"You're being awfully quiet, Kim." Matthew says

when we finally get to the pickup, and he opens the door for me. "What are you thinking about?"

"Oh?" I turn to him surprised. "Nothing really."

But once we're both inside, he pesters me to tell him. "It must sound pretty silly," I say after I've confessed my guilt over Mom doing my laundry.

"No, it's actually sweet. How's your mom doing anyway? You never seem to say much about her."

"We don't really talk about it much," I admit. "And for the most part she seems okay. I mean, she's tired a lot, and I know she takes naps during the day and then goes to bed earlier than usual at night. But she manages to keep everything going at home just like normal."

"So you don't really know what the doctors are saying? Or how her health really is?"

"Not exactly. She still isn't taking any chemo or radiation or anything invasive like that. And she got herself this juicer from the Home Shopping Network, and she thinks that drinking lots of this gross-smelling vegetable juice is going to help her get well sooner. And maybe it is..."

Then there's a fairly long silence as Matthew drives toward downtown. Once he finds a parking space directly in front of the Paradiso (since everyone else is probably still at the game), he finally says something. "Does it bother you to talk about your mom?"

I consider this for a moment. I mean, I want to be honest with him. "Yeah, a little bit..." I finally admit. "But I guess it's just because I don't really know what's going on. It's like I kind of assume that she's mostly okay and that everything is going to be okay eventually...like God really is healing her. I believe that most of the time anyway."

"But not always?"

"Sometimes I wake up in the middle of the night and I'm totally freaked, like having an honest-to-goodness panic attack, where my heart is racing and I'm sweating, and I feel absolutely certain that she's going to die from this. So I pray really, really hard, and I try to have strong faith and to believe that she's going to be healed. And then I feel better. But sometimes I feel like a yo-yo. It's a real up and down kind of thing."

We talk about it some more once we're inside the Paradiso, and Matthew asks good questions. I open up more than usual, and I'm actually surprised at how good it feels to let some of this stuff out.

"It's like I've been suppressing some things," I finally say. "Like whenever I bring anything about my mom up to Natalie, she tells me to have more faith, to pray harder. And I know my dad doesn't want to talk about it. He gets really bummed if I bring up Mom's health or ask a question about a doctor's appointment. And since I hate seeing him like that, well, I just don't talk to him about it much."

Matthew nods. "You can talk to me about it—anytime, Kim."

"Thanks. But the fact is, I get kind of bummed talking about it too. I mean, who knows what's going to happen? She really could get well, you know. God does do miracles."

Then I tell him about Nat's desperate prayer for a Christian boyfriend, going into far more comedic detail than I really should, and we both end up laughing so hard that we're crying, and I actually have to use the restroom for fear of wetting my pants.

"Okay," I finally say after I come back to the table. "You must promise me, swear to me, that you will never let on to Nat that I told you about this. It was so wrong. She's my best friend, and I just made her sound like the village idiot. So wrong..."

He nods. "Yeah, but it was so funny."

"But you promise?"

"Of course, Kim. My lips are sealed."

And so I've come to the conclusion that the reason I really like being with Matthew is because he gets me. He totally gets me. Okay, it doesn't hurt that he looks like one of my favorite actors—Ashton Kutcher—or that he's a good kisser. But even without those surface things, I would still like him. Sure, it might be nice if he was a Christian, but that could happen. Even without being saved, he has a really good heart. And naturally, I am praying for him.

And I can tell that he feels something is missing in his life, whether or not he can admit it himself. I really believe that you can't rush these things anyway. I mean, there was no way I could've come to God any sooner than I did. So why would I expect more of

Matthew? I think patience is the key here.

On another note, I've decided that it's time for me to start doing my own laundry. I plan to bring it up to Mom tomorrow. I need to do it in such a way that I don't offend her. Or maybe she'll just be relieved. Okay, I know it's a pretty small step for most people, but I don't even know how to turn on the washing machine. I wonder if it has a manual or something I can read first.

Saturday, February 11

Note to self: When it comes to doing laundry, less is more.

Now for my laundry rules:

1) Do not overload the machine.

2) Do not put in "extra" soap.

3) If you fail to follow instructions one and two, make sure you have a mop and bucket handy.

4) Do not let Mom know what a mess you made.

Well, at least the laundry room was squeaky clean by the time I got finished—more than six hours after I started! Hopefully next time will go a little smoother.

Tuesday, February 14

I gave Matthew a Valentine's Day card and chocolate heart today. He gave me a red rose. Very romantic. I can't believe how fun it was having a boyfriend on this silly holiday. And I wasn't the only one.

"Ben got me a Valentine," Natalie told me when I ran into her on my way to art.

"That's cool," I said. "So did Matthew."

She kind of frowned then, and I knew it was her disapproving scowl for the fact that I'm hooking up with a heathen. What could I say?

"I hope you're being careful, Kim."

"What does that mean, Nat?" I looked up at her, realizing how her height combined with her disapproval can be a little overwhelming sometimes. But then I should be used to her, right? "Like am I looking both ways before I cross the street? Flossing regularly? What is it you're trying to say?"

"You know what I mean."

I shrugged and tried to look dumb. "Not exactly, Nat. I mean, I am by nature a pretty careful person." Then I glanced at my watch. "I gotta go or I'll be late."

But I was feeling pretty steamed as I went to art. What right does she have to judge me? Who died and made her God anyway? Sometimes I feel like I'm living out a scene from that movie she got so upset over. But then I remind myself that I really do love Natalie, warts and all.

Besides, I know that God expects us to forgive others—seventy times seven, which I've heard is supposed to represent eternity. So there you have it. Nat offends me, and I forgive her again and again and again. I guess that's the reason I picked this particular letter to answer today.

Dear Jamie,

I'm so (verb replaced) ticked at my so-called best friend that all I can think of is getting even. I trusted her and she totally betrayed me. I told her a secret, something really embarrassing, something I've never told anyone, and she went around blabbing this to the entire school. I'm so humiliated I could die. I want to change schools, but my parents won't let me. I've even pretended to be sick. Sometimes I imagine killing this girl. I don't think I really would, but I wish I could hire someone. She has called and e-mailed me a bunch of times, and she claims she only told one person and that was "by accident." But I don't believe her. She says she's sorry, but I don't care. I wish she were dead.

Backstabbed and Angry

Dear Backstabbed,

You have a right to be angry. But after a while, you may want to consider whether or not your anger is helping anything. It's possible that your anger is just making you feel worse. I'm thinking that if you had a secret that private and humiliating, it could mean you really need to talk to a professional (like a school counselor or pastor). Some secrets aren't good to keep inside. But beyond that, you need to talk to your friend. You need to tell her how you feel betrayed and how you can't trust her. You also need to listen to her side of the story. It's possible that you guys will never be friends again. But it's also possible that she's really, really sorry and that you might be able to forgive her and start over. Whether or not you choose to be friends, you should try to forgive her and move on. Because if you don't forgive her, and if you remain angry, you will eventually end up hurting yourself way more than you can ever hurt her.

Just Jamie

Eleven

Monday, February 27

Whoo-hoo! I just had the best weekend ever! On Saturday (which just happened to be my seventeenth birthday), Matthew and I went snowboarding together, and it was totally awesome. We had to get up really early, and I drove my Jeep since it's better on snow than Matthew's old pickup. And when we got up there, the sun was shining and the snow was perfect and we had the greatest time riding all day. I packed us a lunch and a thermos of hot cocoa (to save money and time so we didn't have to wait in the cafeteria line to eat), and as a result we spent every minute possible on the slopes.

Then after the last ride, we loaded up our stuff and headed to the nearby town and ate at this old-fashioned burger joint (Matthew's treat). All in all, it was a very cool birthday, and I'd have to say it's the best date I've ever had in my life.

However, as my dad would say, there was a fly in the ointment (which means that while everything was generally great, one little thing went wrong), and now that I'm home, I'm thinking it was a rather big and nasty fly at that. Here's what happened. We'd just finished our picnic lunch, and I went to use the restroom when I ran into someone from school.

"Kim Peterson!" a slightly familiar voice said as I washed my hands at the sink.

I looked into the mirror to see that Torrey Barnes was standing at the sink right next to me. "Torrey," I said in surprise. "What are you doing here?"

She laughed. "Probably the same thing as you." Then she looked down at my snowboard boots. "Well, actually I'm a skier, not a boarder. Although I've been thinking about trying it out."

"You should," I told her as I dried my hands. "I gave up skiing for boarding after just one day."

She nodded as she applied some lip gloss. "Yeah, I hear it's pretty fun, but my parents are die-hard skiers, and they keep discouraging me from going over to the other side."

"Hey, I've missed you at youth group lately." I fished around in my pocket for my tube of Chapstick.

She sighed loudly. "Yeah, I've kind of missed going to youth group too. But I sort of needed some space, you know what I mean?"

I nodded, thinking about her breakup with Ben. "I guess it's probably hard at first."

Then she looked at me more closely. "You're really good friends with Natalie McCabe, aren't you?"

"Yeah..." Now I considered adding, "I used to be...before she started dating your ex," but fortunately I had the good sense not to say this. But it is true that I've seen a lot less of Nat since she started going out with Ben.

"I was just thinking maybe you should, uh, warn her..." Then she stopped as if she wasn't sure whether to continue or not.

"Warn her?"

Torrey pressed her lips together as if reconsidering.

"Warn her about what?" I persisted.

"Maybe I shouldn't say anything. I mean, it could be taken as gossip, although I'm not sure that it's actually gossip when someone shares firsthand knowledge..."

"What do you mean?" Okay, gossip or no gossip, I was getting pretty curious now.

"Well, it's about Ben. He's really a pretty nice guy, and I guess I just thought that because he was a Christian, well..." Then she gets close enough to whisper in my ear, telling me that Ben isn't as good a Christian as he may appear to be. "He's just like all the other guys. But I got tired of the pressure from him." Then she held up her hand where a small gold ring seemed prominent. "I mean, it's not like I wear this True Love Waits ring for nothing. I take my promises seriously."

I wasn't sure how to respond to that, or why she was even telling me this in the first place. So I just stood there, probably looking pretty stupid, not saying anything.

"Maybe I shouldn't have told you," she said quickly. "But I figured if you're Natalie's friend, well, maybe you should warn her. I know she's a strong Christian too, and I just wouldn't want to see her getting hurt too."

Now talk about turning the tables! Here Nat has been all freaked about me and Matthew, and she's involved with a guy who's just as human as the rest of us. Although in Matthew's defense, he has NOT pressured me about sex—not even once. Okay, not yet anyway. I'm fully aware that the subject could come up and probably will come up. But I also know that I am not ready to have sex. And I have no problem telling him that.

The question is, what do I do about Natalie now? Do I tell her what Torrey said? Or do I just let it go? Let Natalie find out for herself? I must say I'm pretty surprised that Ben's like that, especially since his sister is so totally opposite, but then I guess things like "abstinence" don't exactly run in families. And I know that just because a guy is a Christian, doesn't mean he's perfect either. Anyway, I decide to pray about this thing with Nat, and I ask God to show me what's best to do. And while I feel more peaceful about it, I'm still a little uneasy when it comes to being around Nat.

For the first time since she started dating Ben, I was actually feeling somewhat glad that it's driven a slight wedge between us. I mean, as it is I hardly even see her anymore. And when we talk at school, it's usually pretty brief and shallow. And I can tell by the look in her eyes that she feels kind of guilty for the way she's been treating me—and she should! But today I was pretty much relieved that our conversation was so superficial.

"Did you have a good weekend?" she asked when I saw her by her locker.

I told her about snowboarding with Matthew, and her expression suggested she still questioned this relationship.

"How was your weekend?" I asked before she had a chance to remind me of the dangers of dating a non-Christian.

She smiled. "It was fantastic. Ben and I went to dinner and a movie on Saturday, and he actually came to my church with me and my family yesterday."

"Really?"

"Yeah, he said he wanted to see what a megachurch was like."

"Did he like it?"

She frowned. "Not really. But at least he understands what I go through now."

"I thought you liked your church, Nat."

"I like some things about it, but it's got its drawbacks and I know it's not perfect."

"Do you think any church is?"

"Maybe..."

"Well, I gotta go," I told her since the second bell was about to ring.

"Take care," she called, but I knew what she meant was "be careful." The ironic thing was that's exactly what I wanted to tell her. But how?

So tonight as I'm picking letters for my column, I decide to tackle a couple of the sex ones. The truth is, I usually try to avoid these. But now I'm thinking that maybe I can reach Natalie through Just Jamie. We'll see...

Dear Jamie,

I'm sixteen and have been sexually active for almost a year now. I'm pretty careful, but the possibility of getting pregnant totally freaks me, and I really want to start using some kind of reliable birth control before that happens. But I know if I go to the doctor my parents will find out and go ballistic. I've considered going to one of those free clinics downtown, but they look so sleazy and I'd hate to be seen there by someone. Any suggestions?

Anon

Okay, I'm wondering, does anyone pay attention in health class? I mean, it's not cool to appear too interested in some of the gross stuff that is taught, but I happen to believe that knowledge is power, and just knowing some of the consequences of casual sex motivates me to make some very careful choices. Not that I'm even considering anything. But if I were...

Dear Anon,

Well, since you asked...my first question for you is, what does "sexually active" mean? To me it suggests that you've had sex with more than just one partner. That in itself is a major concern—especially since there is an epidemic of sexually transmitted diseases out there, and the more people you have sex with, the greater the chances you may have contracted one. While getting pregnant should concern you, you should be even more concerned about your health, since some STDs can stay with you for the rest of your life. So whether you go to your family doctor or a free clinic is up to you. I just encourage you to get there soon. And then you may want to reconsider your sex life altogether.

Just Jamie

Dear Jamie,

I've been going with the same guy since last summer. And I'm pretty sure that he's the ONE. I mean, I really love him, and I think he really loves me. But when I was twelve, I made a pledge to save myself for my husband and marriage, and I always thought that I'd stick to it. But now it's five years later, and I'm rethinking the whole thing. Is there anything wrong with having sex with someone you really love and plan to spend the rest of your life with?

Floundering

Dear Floundering,

You sound like a sensitive and thoughtful girl who's gotten a little confused lately. Here are my questions for you: 1) You say that you're "pretty sure he's the ONE," but are you absolutely positive? 2) You made a promise that was important to you, but now you're ready to toss it aside? 3) You say that you "think" he really loves you, but are you totally sure?

This is the deal: It sounds like you must be about seventeen, and in my opinion (and since you asked), that is way too young to make a lifetime commitment. I guess you need to ask yourself how you would feel if you broke your pledge, had sex with your boyfriend, and then he dumped you? Because, whether you want to hear this or not, statistics prove that's exactly what will happen. If you really care about yourself and your feelings and future, you should honor your promise and wait. I really don't think you'll be sorry—not in the long run.

Just Jamie

Twelve

Saturday, March 11

I think Nat and I are having some kind of standoff. And it's probably mostly my fault, but I'm so tired of her putting down Matthew and acting like Ben is such a saint. Worse than that, she's more and more obsessed with fitting in with Ben's friends lately. And it's like I don't even know her anymore.

"Is something wrong between you and Natalie?" my mom asked me today. She wasn't feeling too well this morning, so I took her in a tray with breakfast—well, just toast and one of her weird juice concoctions and some green tea, but she appreciated it.

I played with the edge of her comforter as I sat on the bed, wondering how to best answer her. "Sort of..."

"Seems like she hasn't been around in weeks." Mom sipped her tea then looked at me. "Did you two have a fight?"

"Not exactly. More like a disagreement. And now we're not really talking much."

"Want to tell me about it?"

I considered this. On one hand I don't like to leave Mom out, but on the other hand I don't like to worry her either. Dad's been kind of protective of her lately, and I'm not really sure how much she can take these days. Not that we ever discuss it much—it's kind of like we're still just tiptoeing around and pretending that nothing's wrong. Most of the time I actually believe it too, but looking at her, still in her pink flannel nightgown and her pale face, I wasn't so sure.

"It has to do with boyfriends," I ventured.

Mom smiled. "Ah-hah."

So I went ahead and told her about the way Natalie constantly disapproves of Matthew and how I'm completely fed up with it. "It's not that her boyfriend is so great. I mean, I've heard some things about him that are a little questionable, if you ask me."

Her brows lifted slightly. "Did you tell Natalie these, uh, things?"

"No." Then I studied her expression. "Do you think I should?"

She sighed. "No, not necessarily. You already know how it feels to have someone coming down on your boyfriend. And has Natalie's disapproval changed how you feel about Matthew?"

I shook my head. "Not really. If anything it probably

makes me more defensive of him. He really is a nice guy, Mom."

She nodded. "And Natalie might feel the same way about her guy too."

I had to smile. "Thanks, Mom."

"For what?"

"For being so wise."

She smiled. "Maybe we do get smarter with age."

"You're not that old, Mom."

"I feel old today, Kim."

I didn't know what to say to that.

Then she smiled again. "But this breakfast is just what I needed, sweetheart. And I think it's going to be a sunny day today. I'd like to plant some annuals."

"Need any help?"

"That'd be lovely."

So I spent a couple of hours helping Mom to plant petunias and pansies and marigolds this afternoon. Mostly she directed me from where she was sitting in a sunny spot on the porch. But I didn't' mind doing the actual work, and to my surprise it didn't look half bad by the time I was done.

I was just packing some soil around the last petunia when I heard my mom calling out "hello" to someone. I looked up in time to see Natalie climbing out of their old Toyota pickup with some bags in her hands. Judging by the colors and logos, I could see they probably contained clothing. Naturally, this aroused my curiosity since Nat is normally pretty tight with money. Although now that I think of it, I have noticed that her wardrobe's been improving since she started dating Ben.

"Hey," Nat called back. "How's it going?"

"Good," my mom returned. "Isn't it a beautiful day?"

To my surprise Natalie started walking toward us; I expect this was on account of my mom. In fact, I wasn't even sure that Nat had spotted me from where I was still hunched over on the far side of the porch as I spread the last of the mulch around my recently planted blooms. I stood up and brushed my dirty hands on my overalls and said, "Hey, Nat."

"Oh, Kim," she said. "I didn't even see you. What's up?"

"I'm playing gardener today." I came out of the flower bed and over to the porch steps. "Looks like you've been doing some shopping."

She seemed kind of embarrassed by this. "Just a few spring things I picked up at Nordies."

Now I almost questioned this—I mean, Nat's the one who always says Nordstrom's way too expensive—but I kept my mouth shut. However, I'm sure she was reading my mind.

"They were on sale," she said quickly as if to explain.

I nodded and went over to stand next to where Mom was sitting in the wicker rocker.

"How are you feeling, Mrs. Peterson?"

"Wonderful, Natalie." Mom took in a deep breath and

slowly exhaled. "With the sunshine and the flowers planted...well, it's been a perfectly lovely day."

"Are you tired?" I asked suddenly, realizing that she usually has an afternoon nap and it was already nearly four.

She slowly stood up. "Yes, I think I'll go catch a little rest before your dad gets back. You girls go ahead and chat without me."

Okay, I knew what she was getting at, but there was no way I was going to force Natalie to stick around and "chat." We both watched silently as my mom slowly went into the house.

"Everything okay with you guys?" Nat finally said after the door shut behind my mom.

I turned and looked at her, fighting to cover the exasperation that was building inside of me. "What do you mean by okay?"

"I mean, how's your mom doing, Kim. You know I'm still praying for her. I'm still believing for a miracle."

I studied Nat now. Just then everything about her seemed entirely different to me—like I didn't even know her anymore. And yet she seemed slightly familiar too. "Thanks," I told her. "We appreciate it."

"She looks pretty good," Nat continued in her normal upbeat and positive way. "Like she's getting better."

"She doesn't have a lot of energy," I said, ever the realist.

"But she does seem to be in good spirits," Nat

continued. "I guess some healings just take time. We have to be patient and keep praying and believing."

I just shrugged and looked away.

"Are you still trusting God with this, Kim?"

I looked back at her. Who was she to question my faith? After all, this was my mother we were discussing here. But I didn't say anything.

"You've got to trust Him completely, Kim. You've got to believe that God is healing her. It will strengthen your prayers."

I just sighed and sat in the rocker. "Yeah, whatever."

Natalie looked concerned now. "You're not falling away from God, are you, Kim? I mean, that can happen when you spend too much time with nonbelievers, and I know how Matthew is a pretty big influence in your life. I still pray for you guys and that he'll get saved."

I felt like I was a teakettle, and the heat beneath me kept getting hotter and hotter, and I was seriously worried that I was going to blow. But I kept my lips sealed tightly. Maybe it's my Asian genes, who knows, but I guess I have pretty good self-control. Well, most of the time anyway. Still, it was all I could do not to explode all over her.

"Are you mad at me, Kim?"

Of course, Nat's known me long enough to realize that not only was I mad, but I was suppressing something as well. Even so I was determined not to give her the satisfaction of seeing me lose my cool. That would probably just help convince her that she was right, that I had fallen away from God's grace and that it was all due to my sinful relationship with the heathen Matthew. No way was I going there.

"I'm not mad at you, Nat," I said rather coolly. "In a way, I feel kind of sorry for you."

She blinked. "You're sorry for me?"

"Yeah." I stood up now, leaning against one of the posts and just evenly looking at her. "I mean, you've been out shopping, I'm sure to impress your new friends, but I know you can't afford it. And Nordstroms? You used to hate that store. What's up with that?"

"For your information, my dad finally sent me some money."

"Really?" Of course, I wanted to ask why she's wasting it on stupid clothes that probably cost way too much and will be out of style by next week anyway. Especially when she should be saving it for college or something more important, like helping out on her mom's credit card bills, which last I heard were really bringing her down. But I simply said, "That was nice of him."

"Yeah, it was."

"So how are things with you and Ben?" I asked, actually feeling curious about how their relationship was going.

She shrugged. "Okay."

"Just okay?"

She looked away, and I could tell she was feeling a little uncomfortable like she did not want to have this conversation.

"Sorry," I said quickly, hiding my pleasure at hitting a nerve. "It's none of my business."

"How are things with you and Matthew?" she said.

"Great," I told her with a big smile. "Things couldn't be better."

She seemed to study me then, as if not entirely convinced that everything really was great between Matthew and me. "Well, good for you. But just the same, Kim, you better be careful."

I felt my teeth grinding together as she said those all-too-familiar words. And despite my resolve to just chill and not get all riled, I couldn't stop myself. "You better be careful too, Nat." And the tone of my voice was not very loving or kind and certainly not a bit Christlike. But it was too late. It was out there.

Her eyes narrowed slightly. "What do you mean by that?"

Now I realized I could stop, but it's like there was this mean streak running through me, or maybe the devil made me do it. But I kept on going. "I mean, from what I've heard, you'd better be careful too. Just because a guy is a Christian doesn't mean that he's perfect."

"Who have you been talking to?"

I didn't answer her, but I could tell by her expression that I'd really hit a touchy spot. I just folded my arms across my front and watched her, and she was almost squirming. Okay, that might've been my evil imagination.

"Come on, Kim. What have you heard?"

"You know if we were still friends, and if we had the

kind of trust that we used to have, I might be able to tell you. As it is, I'm sorry I even opened my mouth right now." Okay, guilt kicked in and I softened up a little. And I could tell by her eyes that she was seriously troubled. "And the truth is," I said with sincerity, "I still care about you, and I really wouldn't want to see you getting hurt. So seriously, why don't you take your own advice for a change, okay? You be careful too."

Well, she was pretty speechless after that. And I was feeling a little sorry that I'd opened my big fat mouth. So much for that Asian self-control gene. Anyway, we both said an awkward good-bye, and she headed back over to her house. The way she walked reminded me of a kicked dog, and I knew that I was the one who'd done the kicking. And even though I should be feeling like slug slime, I was feeling just a little bit smug. Like one point for Kim. How pathetic is that?

Okay, I do still care about her, and I do wish we were still friends. Just the same, I have to admit that I got some satisfaction out of hurting her just now. And I know that was totally wrong, and that I'm a pretty poor excuse for a Christian, and I'm sure God wasn't too pleased with me today. But I'm not exactly sure what I should do to remedy this. Besides confessing my sins to God, which I've already done. I suppose I'll need to do something with Nat too. But I try to forget about this as I answer some letters for the column. It just figures that one of the ones I pick out is about friendship.

Dear Jamie,

My best friend has really changed this year. We used to have fun together, but now all she thinks about is losing weight. She counts every single calorie and exercises all the time. And now she's starting to get on me about my weight too. And even though I could probably stand to lose a few pounds, I'm not exactly obese, if you know what I mean, I don't really appreciate her comments. But what really gets me is that she's already really, really skinny, and yet she keeps saying she's "so disgustingly fat." It just makes me want to scream. At the same time, I really do love her and I want to be her friend, but she's making me totally crazy with her obsession over weight. What should I do?

Worried

Dear Worried,

You have good reason to be worried. It sounds like your friend might be anorexic or at the very least toying with the idea. Have you asked her about this specifically? Of course, most anorexics won't admit their secret to even their closest friends. But if your friend is underweight and still focused on caloric intake and overexercising, she's probably struggling with it. Anorexia is like any other addiction—it's impossible to quit without admitting you have a problem then getting some help. Encourage your friend to talk openly with you and then to get help. If she refuses, consider talking to her parents. Often parents are the last ones to know. But I hope you can continue being her friend, because it sounds as if she really needs you. Good luck.

Just Jamie

Thirteen

Friday, March 17

Dad surprised us earlier this week by announcing that he was taking some vacation time next week (which is also spring break for me). "And I've booked a cruise," he announced, as if that should be the happiest news ever. "I found a great deal online, made a fairly low offer, and it was accepted. We're going!"

"You and mom?" I asked hopefully since I really wanted to stick around and do some things with Matthew next week. We'd already made some tentative plans.

"For all three of us," he said cheerfully.

"Of course," said Mom, "we couldn't leave you home alone, sweetheart."

"Oh, but you could," I began, then seeing the disappointment in her eyes, I instantly reneged. "What kind of cruise?" I said quickly, as if I was really interested. It turns out it is a Caribbean cruise and something that Mom has always wanted to do. Of course, this is news to me. Still, I have no reason to doubt Dad.

"You could invite a friend, Kim. It doesn't cost much more for another person," said Dad. "Wouldn't Natalie love to come along?"

Well, under normal circumstances, I'm sure that she would. But understandably, Dad's a little out of touch when it comes to me and my friends lately. Not that I have so many friends beyond Nat. And I doubt that they'd want me to invite Matthew, although I did consider this possibility for a few very brief seconds. "I think Nat's busy next week," I finally said to Dad. But Mom seemed to see right through me as she put her hand on my shoulder in what I'm sure she thought was a comforting gesture.

"Well, it'll just be the three of us then," said Dad. "But don't worry, Kim, we'll make a good time of it."

Okay, I know this whole spur-of-the-moment vacation thing has to do with Mom's illness. I know that Dad is thinking our time with her is limited and that she's not going to get better. And I have to admit that she doesn't really seem to be improving much. I mean, she has good days and bad days...but she usually seems worse after visiting the doctor.

Still, she drinks her veggie drinks and green tea and several other strange-looking herbal remedies she picks up at the health food store on a weekly basis. So who knows? And despite what Natalie thinks about my faith or lack of it, I am still praying for a miracle, and I don't even mind if it's an eleventh-hour miracle. I do believe that God can make her well—in His timing.

Matthew was disappointed when he heard that I would be gone a whole week, but he was encouraging too. "Of course you gotta go, Kim. This is a once-in-a-lifetime deal. Just go and have fun and come back with a great tan."

So Mom and I did a little vacation shopping on Thursday night, but she wore out early, and we decided we might just buy some "summer" clothes during our trip anyway. Then Matthew and I went out tonight, and now it's time to pack and finish up a couple letters to run in my column while we're gone.

Dear Jamie,

My parents keep insisting that I go to college right after I graduate from high school next year. The thing is, I don't have any idea what I'd like to do with my life. I keep asking them if I could just put college off for a year, maybe work and travel and stuff—you know, until I really know what I want to do. But they are throwing fits. They say if I don't go to college following graduation that I never will. I don't agree. So we decided I should write to you (since they think you're very mature for a teenager) and see what you say. Help.

Undecided

Dear Undecided,

Tell your parents "thanks" for the compliment but that I side with you on this question. Seriously, why waste money on college if your heart and your head aren't into it? Working and traveling are a form of education too. I think you're right; a year off might really help to ground you and make you see what you'd like to do with your life so that you appreciate a college education and make the most of it.

Just Jamie

Dear Jamie,

I love watching makeover shows like "The Swan," and my greatest dream is to be on a show like this myself. My mom keeps telling me I should be happy with my looks, but I think I could look so much better with a little work. What's your opinion on plastic surgery, and how old do you think a person should be before they go under the knife?

Ugly Duckling

Dear Duckling,

I refuse to call you "ugly" since I've never met you, and I seriously doubt that you are ugly. And while I think an occasional makeover show can be entertaining, they also have very little to do with reality. I'd like to see a show that follows up with people after their exterior appearance is so transformed that their own family hardly recognizes them. I'm sure they must still have some challenges to face. And what if they get so obsessed with their looks that the rest of their life goes down the toilet and everyone starts to hate them for being so vain and superficial? I think we all need to learn to like ourselves—just the way we are. And if there are moderate ways to improve our looks and if we're doing it for the right reasons (not to impress our friends!), then maybe it's just fine. Beauty is very subjective—meaning that it all depends on your personal taste. I think that's why God made us all different. So instead of turning ourselves into cookie-cutter images of the latest fashion icon, why not take a moment to enjoy our differences?

Just Jamie

It's funny how reassured I felt after answering that letter. Because despite my "mature" sounding response, I've been known to worry about my looks too. I've had lots of times when I wished I were taller, thinner, and less Asian. But I'm thankful I never tried to change anything.

My self-esteem has improved a lot by being with Matthew. For one thing, he totally loves that I'm Korean. He says I'm exotic and beautiful, and I think he really means it. He also likes that I'm petite, and he even picks me up and carries me around just to make the point, which is a mix between embarrassing and fun. Okay, I don't honestly see "exotic" and "beautiful" when I look in the mirror, but I do see myself in a more positive light.

That is, unless I'm trying on swimsuits like I did last night. That was pretty torturous. But if I squinted just right and imagined a little tan...well, it might be okay. Besides, who's going to be around to see me during the cruise anyway? Well, other than my parents and a bunch of old people. So why worry?

Sunday, March 26

The cruise was actually pretty fun. To my surprise there were a number of teens cruising with their parents too, and I actually made a couple of friends to hang with. One girl, Audrey, was an adoptee from Korea, and we found we had quite a bit in common. We even exchanged e-mail addresses and plan to stay in touch. She's really been spending a lot of time searching for her birth mom lately. I told her that I'd kind of "been there and done that" but that I still get curious sometimes.

I didn't mention to Audrey that my mom has cancer and that her precarious health might have something to do with my general lack of interest in finding my birth mom these days. Somehow I just didn't want to go there. I didn't want Audrey to feel sorry for me or uncomfortable about how to act. And selfishly, I suppose I just wanted to be carefree and have fun.

As usual, Dad and I tried to wear our sunny faces, pretending that all is well with our little family. But Mom was moving pretty slowly. And she spent a fair amount of time just resting on the deck in her favorite lounge chair and a fat novel, which I have a feeling she didn't actually read. Whenever we questioned this or whether she wanted to go on shore and do something, she always replied that looking at the ocean and soaking up the sun with a good book was "perfectly heavenly." Then she'd encourage us to go off and take some excursion. "Then you can tell me all about it during dinnertime." And so we would.

I suspect that she spent some time napping while we were gone, but she was always dressed for dinner and wearing a smile by the time we got back. In fact, I actually started to think that everything was just fine and that she wasn't sick at all. But she seemed pretty worn out by the time we got off our last flight today. She slept all the way home from the airport. But she told us both that she'd had a fantastic time and that the cruise was all she'd hoped for and more. So I guess Dad was right to book it after all.

Just the same, I'm so glad to be home. If we hadn't gotten in so late, I probably would've done something with Matthew tonight. But we talked on the phone, and he assured me that he desperately missed me. So I guess all is well. I have to admit to some insecurities while I was away, imagining that he'd meet some wonderful girl who would steal his heart away during my week's absence. Just call me paranoid and insecure. Although all I have to do is read the Just Jamie mail to be reminded that things like that really do happen.

Dear Jamie,

How long does it take to heal from a broken heart? Or does the pain ever go away? It's been two weeks since my boyfriend of almost one whole year broke up with me, and I am still totally devastated. I so did not see this coming. I thought things were just great between us. So great that, after eight months of refusing him, I finally gave in and surrendered my virginity. I really thought we'd be together forever, and I can't believe that he broke up with me or that he already has a new girlfriend. Sometimes I get up in the morning and just wish I were dead. When will this pain go away?

Brokenhearted

Dear Brokenhearted,

First of all, I am so sorry you're in such pain. And I have a feeling there's no definite time frame for when it will go away. Now I know you're probably not going to like my next advice, but I think you have to put this guy out of your mind, get out and do something new, and try to forget him. Maybe you could take up a new hobby, or volunteer somewhere, or plan a special trip. Do something healthy to distract you from the pain. Prayer can help too. And whatever you do, make sure that you don't give away your heart so easily next time. Save it for a guy who really deserves you.

Just Jamie

Fourteen

Saturday, April 1

"I have some good news for you, Kim," my dad told me when he came in the house today. Being a newspaper editor, it's not unusual that he'd been at the office on a Saturday.

"What's that?" I asked without even looking up from the music sheet I was studying, trying to memorize a new piece for our upcoming spring concert.

"You've been syndicated."

I looked up to see that he was still wearing his soaking wet raincoat. "What?"

"Your Just Jamie column has been syndicated."

"You mean other newspapers are actually picking it up?"

He nodded with a smile as he removed his raincoat, gave it shake, then hung it on the hall tree. "It's really pouring out there."

I frowned at him now. "Is this an April Fools' Day joke, Dad?"

He laughed as he hung up his hat. "No, not at all. Isn't it great?"

"Seriously? I've really been syndicated?"

"It's only about a dozen other papers, and the deal is to test the column for a couple months to see how it goes."

I jumped up and hugged him. "That's awesome, Dad! It's almost like being famous." Then I stopped. "But of course, I can't tell anyone, can I?"

"Not really."

"That's what I thought."

"But if it keeps going and if other papers pick it up..." Dad looked so pleased that I thought he was about to burst at the seams. "Well, it's as if you've already launched a little writing career, Kim."

"That is so cool!"

"That also means you'll be making more money."

"No way!"

He nodded. "But don't start making any expensive plans just yet. I suggest you put it into savings and see how it goes with the other papers."

"Sure. I just wish I could tell someone the good news." More than anything, I would've loved to call Matthew just then.

"Why don't you tell your mom?"

"I will, Dad. As soon as she gets up from her nap. We made some black bean soup in the Crock-Pot this morning. I think it might be ready if you're hungry."

"Sounds great."

So I've been syndicated, I keep telling myself, feeling famous and happy and yet slightly frustrated that I can't tell anyone. Well, other than Mom. And I have to admit that it was pretty fun telling her.

"That is fantastic, Kim!" she told me after she heard the news this afternoon. "And I'm not a bit surprised. I've been very impressed with your answers, and I've even heard other people, mostly moms, who think Just Jamie is wonderful. It's all I can do to keep my mouth closed and not brag that it's written by my own daughter."

"I know how you feel. I'd love to tell the world right now."

She smiled. "Well, maybe that's what keeps it so genuine and helpful—the fact that you can write it anonymously. If everyone knew it was you, you might have a hard time being so honest and forthright in it."

I'm sure that she's exactly right. I mean, I'm not sure how I'd answer the following letter if everyone in town knew that Kim Peterson was Just Jamie.

Dear Jamie,

I had sex before, and I asked God to forgive me, but I have a new boyfriend who understands my situation and really cares about me. He says he's willing to wait with me, but when we're together it is really hard to wait. Can you help me stay true to God?

Trying

Dear Trying,

You say "when we're together it is really hard to wait," which may be your clue. I guess I have to wonder what you're doing when you are together. I mean, if you're all by yourselves and kissing and stuff, well, sure it's going to be hard to wait. It's like if you were on a diet and you spent all your time at McDonald's, it might be hard to lose weight. If you and this guy want to continue your relationship, I suggest you do things with groups of people. Avoid those times and places that tempt you. And if you want to stay true to God, you better ask God to lead you.

Just Jamie

Okay, the reason I'm struggling with this particular letter is that I feel a little conviction coming on myself. I mean, Matthew and I aren't considering having sex—at least I'm not—but we do spend quite a bit of time together, and sometimes I think we get a little carried away in our make-out sessions. And I suppose the more you push things, the easier it would be to just give in. So maybe I'll have to take my own advice and suggest that Matthew and I start doing things with others and in groups. At least I convinced him to come to youth group with me tonight. And it should be fun since it's an April Fools' party, and we're supposed to dress up in goofy costumes.

Wednesday, April 5

Matthew invited me to go to the prom with him today! Now, I fully realize that if I hadn't been asked to the prom, I probably would just act like, hey, the prom's just a silly formal function anyway, and who cares whether you go or not? But the truth is, I've always wanted to go to the prom, and I actually thought I might never get the chance. So I am feeling kind of thrilled. Of course, I was all chill about it when I told Matthew, "Sure, that sounds cool."

But it was fun when I got home and told my mom. She was sitting in the living room reading her Bible, and I could tell by the shadows under her eyes and the creases in her forehead that she wasn't feeling well. This seems to be more the case lately, and I guess it's got me worried. But she really brightened up when I told her the good news.

"Oh, Kim." She set down her Bible and clapped her hands. "That's wonderful. When is it?"

"Saturday, April 29."

Her face grew serious as she considered this, and I could almost see her counting off the days until then. "That's about three weeks. I suppose that's plenty of time to get everything together."

I smiled. "Oh, I could probably get it together within a week if I had to."

"Well, let's not waste any time," she said suddenly. "Why don't we go shopping this weekend before the dresses get all picked over? Maybe we could even go into the city where the selection is better."

"Really?" I said in surprise. "You feel up to that?"

"Of course," she said happily. "It's not every day my little girl gets to go to the prom!"

So now I'm thinking maybe I was just reading more into it. Maybe Mom was just needing her nap and not really getting sicker. I know she goes to the doctor on Friday though. I hope she doesn't come home feeling all discouraged. Although a shopping excursion might cheer her up, if it doesn't wear her out. But maybe I should run this by Dad too. He might not like the idea of her going to the city to shop for prom dresses with me.

Saturday, April 8

As it turned out, Dad decided to drive Mom and me to the city today. He even got off work early to do this. I protested at first, not sure that I wanted a guy along. "It's for your mom's sake, Kim," he told me when we were alone yesterday. "She really wants to do this with you, but I know she's not very strong. I want her to be as comfortable as possible, and she can even nap in the car if she needs to."

But to our surprise, Mom was more energetic than usual. Dad thinks it may have to do with her new pain pills, but I think maybe she's making a turn around—maybe God is finally healing her.

For starters we went to a nice restaurant for lunch,

and Mom surprised us both by eating a small sirloin steak and a baked potato. It's the most we've seen her eat at one sitting in weeks. And to be honest, it had me a little worried because I thought she might feel sick to her stomach later, but she didn't.

I had already decided that I couldn't be too picky about my dress. There's no way I was going to drag Mom from store to store trying to find some absolutely perfect but nonexistent dress. I mean, there are times when you have to settle.

But after one store where absolutely nothing was right, I felt a little discouraged. It seemed like everything was strapless, backless, and without much more coverage than swimwear. In other words, it wasn't me. It's not like I'm afraid to show a little skin; I just don't like the idea of having my dress falling off or exposing any personal parts—especially not at something as public as a prom!

"Don't worry," Mom assured me as we went into the second store. "There's got to be a dress that's right for you, Kim. And we'll find it if it takes all day."

I exchanged a glance with Dad that was meant to reassure him that I had no intention of taking all day. Then I shot up a little "please, God, help me find a dress that'll be okay for the prom" prayer.

After a couple of racks of formal gowns that were all wrong, I was ready to give up, but Mom called, "Over here, Kim."

I went to the back of the store to see that she'd

found another rack. Unfortunately it turned out to be a more expensive selection of designer gowns, but it wasn't long before Mom pulled out a turquoise blue dress that was made out of this really exquisite fabric. Not only that, but it had straps, and although the back was cut down a little, it wasn't nearly as low as most of them.

She held up the dress. "I think it's your size too."

"Maybe, but it's probably too long."

The next thing I knew, the saleslady was leading me into the dressing room. And before long I had it on. When I looked in the mirror, I could see that it was really quite nice. Its style was similar to some of the strapless gowns I actually think look pretty on some girls, but not quite right for me, and having those thin little straps over my shoulders made me feel a lot better. And if I stood on my toes, pretending to have on heels, I could see that the length and uneven hem was going to be just fine.

When I stepped out of the dressing room, Mom, who had been seated in a comfy looking chair, actually stood up and clapped her hands. "That's absolutely beautiful, Kim!" She came closer to see it better. "That color with your skin tone is just gorgeous."

I looked at myself in the big three-way mirror, and whether it was the soft lighting, my mom's enthusiasm, or the bit of tan that still remained after our cruise, I had to agree with her. It did look good.

"Very pretty," Dad said from where he was standing off to one side and obviously not feeling too comfortable in this very female-focused setting.

"I forgot to look at the price." I turned my head to see if I could spy a tag, which I couldn't.

"Don't worry about it, Kim," said Dad. "The dress is perfect, and I'm sure it can't be too much."

I kind of frowned. "Don't be too sure, Dad." I'd already done a little research online and knew that formal dresses could be outrageously expensive.

"It's lovely on you," said the saleslady. "As if it were made for you."

"That's it," said Mom. "We're taking it!"

Without protesting, I went back to the room, carefully removed the gown, and replaced it on its hanger. But as I zipped it up, I looked at the tag. Gulp! It was way more than I had planned on.

I carried the dress back out and sighed loudly. "It's really expensive. I think we should keep looking."

"No," Mom said firmly. "I think we should get it."

Dad nodded, although I suspect he was curious about the price and might have balked if he'd had a chance to see it before the saleslady happily rang it up, wrapped it in tissue, then zipped it into a long garment bag.

"I know you'll be happy with it," she assured me. For that price, I was thinking, I better be ecstatic in it.

"I'm so happy," Mom said as we went to the car. I'd told them that I could look for shoes later or possibly find a pair online. "That dress is absolutely perfect on you, Kim."

Then to my relief she napped as Dad drove us

home. And now as I sit here, looking at the dress hanging on my closet door, I can't argue that it's gorgeous. And despite the fact that we barely talk anymore, I can't help myself. I pick up the phone and call Natalie.

"What's up?" she asks with obvious surprise.

"I know it's weird," I tell her, suddenly wondering why I've done this. "But I just got the most gorgeous prom dress and—"

"You're going to the prom?"

"Yeah," I say with a tone that probably sounds like 'duh,' although I don't mean to offend her. "Aren't you?"

"Ben hasn't asked me...yet."

"Oh."

"So you already got a dress?" she says with what sounds like genuine interest. "What's it like?"

"You want to come see it?"

"Sure, I'll be over in a few minutes."

And to my complete astonishment, Nat comes over, and I try on my dress at her urging, and she totally approves. "It's beautiful, Kim." And before I know it, I'm back in my jeans, and we're sitting on my bed and talking just like the old days.

"I've missed you," she says.

"Me too."

"How's it going?"

I shrug, unsure of what she means. "Okay, I guess."

"I mean, how's your mom doing?"

"Well, she's slowed down a lot. But she went

shopping with Dad and me today, and we were surprised at how she hung in there." I don't mention her new pain pills.

"Maybe God is healing her." Nat nods. "I'm still praying for her. And I've been thinking God might want to drag this all out so that our faith will grow, you know?"

"Maybe."

"How are things with you and Matthew?" she asks now.

"Good. How about you and Ben?"

She looks down at the throw pillow she has cradled in her lap. "Okay, I guess."

"You guess?"

Then she looks up at me, and there are tears in her eyes.

"What is it, Nat?"

"Oh, nothing."

I'm tempted to push her, urging her to get whatever is wrong out in the open, but I also realize that this is the first time we've really talked in weeks. I don't want to scare her away.

Then she looks at her watch. "I should probably go. I need to get ready for youth group."

"Do you need a ride or anything? Matthew and I are going tonight."

"No. Ben's picking me up."

"Oh, good." I feel somewhat relieved to know that she and Ben are still together. I was worried that he'd broken up with her, and now she was brokenhearted about it. Even so, I can tell something is troubling her as I walk her to the door. "If you ever need to talk," I say hesitantly then sort of laugh, "well, you know where I live."

Then to my surprise she gives me a big hug. "Yeah, I do. Thanks, Kim."

It's still almost an hour before youth group, and I decide to answer a letter for my new syndicated column. Unfortunately it's a really tough letter, and I feel very sorry for the writer. Hopefully he or she has reached a turning point. But Burnt and Scared is definitely going on my prayer list.

Dear Jamie,

This is a really hard letter to write because this will be the first time I've admitted this to anyone, but I think I have a drug problem. I started taking diet pills last summer because I thought it would help me lose weight. I really liked the high I got from them, but after a couple of months it kind of wore off. So I began sneaking my mom's antidepressants, and the high was even better, but I knew she would figure it out. So I started buying pills from a guy I met at a party. And it's like I can't stop now. I've used up all my savings and have even stolen money and things from my parents. I'm really freaked and don't know what to do. Do you think I'm an addict? Help!

Burnt and Scared

Dear Burnt and Scared,

Like with any addiction, admitting you have a problem is the first step. And you definitely have a problem. Yes, my guess is you are an addict since you appear to be unable to stop. You need to get help now. If you can't admit this to your parents yet, make an appointment with a drug counselor and then go to it. It won't be easy to do this, but it will be a LOT easier than continuing to live in the nightmare that drug addiction creates. The good news is that you haven't been addicted for years, like some, and the sooner you get help, the sooner you will begin to feel better. Good luck!

Just Jamie

Fifteen

Monday, April 10

I'm thinking it's just a normal Monday morning—especially nice because the sun is out, and it actually feels as if spring may really be here to stay now—and then I run into Natalie right before first period, and her face looks like a train wreck.

"What's wrong?" I ask.

Then she grabs me and drags me off to the bathroom where she completely falls apart. "B–Ben—" She gasps then stops as a girl comes in and gives us a strange look.

"What happened?" I ask after the girl goes into a stall. "Has he been hurt? A car wreck? What?"

"No–no," she blubbers, going for the paper towels to wipe her face with. "Let's get out of here," she says quickly, grabbing me again.

The next thing I know, we're outside and I hear the

bell ringing, which means I'm late for my AP history which is probably not too serious since my grades are up and I'm not usually late.

"What is going on, Nat?" I demand as we both sit on the cement steps. "Talk to me. What happened to Ben?" Now I'm preparing myself for the worst. He has brain cancer or he's in a coma or—

"He broke up with me!" she exclaims like that's the end of life as we know it. And maybe it is for her, but I'm not so sure I think it's worthy of all this drama myself. Even so, I manage to conceal my disappointment in her theatrics and ask her what happened.

She takes in a deep breath, I'm sure to steady herself, and begins. "I kind of knew it was coming... I could tell something wasn't, well, right, you know..."

"I kind of sensed that on Saturday," I say, hoping to encourage her to spill her story as quickly as possible.

"Well, you know, we were at youth group, 'cause we saw you and Matthew there. And even though Ben was acting kind of different, everything seemed pretty much okay when he took me home. I thought we were just fine..."

"And?" I probe.

Now Nat is choking up again, and I have to wait for her to get it together. Still, I resist the urge to check my watch. I may have to just give up on AP history for today.

"So...he never called me yesterday, and well, I

thought that was kind of weird because we usually talk almost every day. And you know how he's been picking me up for school..."

"Yeah, I see his car almost every morning. In fact, I thought I saw it there today."

"Well, he picked me up, but on the way to school, he told me that he knew God was telling him to break up with me. Just like that!" Now she bursts into tears again, and I put my arms around her and hug her for what seems like several minutes.

"I'm sorry, Nat. That's gotta hurt."

She sniffs and wipes her nose on the crumpled piece of paper towel that she brought from the bathroom. "It does."

Now I'm not sure what to say. I mean, I've never been in the position of having my heart broken, but I have a feeling that I'd feel pretty bad if Matthew broke up with me. Maybe I wouldn't be as devastated as Nat, but then she really went after Ben, and she's been through some losses with her dad leaving and stuff, so I probably don't know what it feels like to be in her shoes.

"The thing I don't get is—like how does Ben know that God's telling him to break up with me but I don't hear God saying a single word about that to me?"

"I don't know..." And I really don't. The truth is, I'm never sure what to think when I hear people saying, 'God told me' about something. That never really happens to me. I mean, I get a sense of things sometimes and I think it's from God, but I would never say, 'God told me.' That just seems too presumptuous.

"I thought Ben was the one, Kim." She starts crying again. "I seriously did. I mean, he's so stable and steady. And I really like his family. And it seemed as if they liked me. I just really thought that he and I would be together always. And when I was at their house and saw all the wedding stuff going on for Caitlin, I imagined that it was going to be like that for Ben and me someday..."

"Seriously?" I study Nat and try not to appear too shocked. "You really thought you and Ben would get married?" Now this actually reminds me of some of the pathetic letters I've received for my column, and I always wonder what planet are these girls from? Who gets married in high school? That is just so weird.

"I know you think it's stupid."

"No, that's not it. I guess I just don't get it."

"That's because you're so grounded, Kim. It's like you were born all grown up. Maybe it has to do with being adopted from Korea."

I have to laugh at that. "Maybe...but I doubt it."

"So I guess you were right, huh?"

"About what?"

"Don't you want to say, 'I told you so'?"

"About what?"

"You told me to be careful that day. Remember when you were working in the yard and we kind of got into a snit? You told me to take my own advice and be careful."

"Oh, yeah. So you wouldn't get hurt."

"Well, now I'm hurt."

"But you'll get over it, Nat. I know it seems like the end of the world now. But it's because it just happened. The wound is all fresh and sore. But you'll feel better—"

"I'll never feel better."

Okay, now I remember the Scripture about crying with those who cry and laughing with those who laugh, and I'm not doing such a great job right now. So I nod and say, "It must feel totally lousy, Nat. I can't even imagine how I'd feel if Matthew broke up with me. But I know I would be really sad, and I would be crying too."

She looks up at me with surprise. "You would?"

"Of course! I really like Matthew, and we've been together for almost six months. It would really hurt if he dumped me."

"So you are human."

I roll my eyes. "Yeah. I guess I just hide it sometimes. Maybe it's my Asian genes or something."

She nods and wipes her nose again. "Yeah, maybe."

"Really, Nat, I'm sorry that Ben hurt you like this. Do you want me to go beat him up?"

She almost smiles now. This used to be an old joke when someone would pick on one of us (mostly me for being different), and Nat would say, 'Do you want me to go beat her up?' Then she gets a thoughtful look on her face. "No, I don't want you to go beat him up, Kim, but maybe you could talk to him."

"Talk to him?" Now I'm not too sure about this.

"Maybe you could just ask him why."

"Why?" I say weakly.

"Why he broke up with me."

"Oh."

Now she frowns. "Oh, forget it. I shouldn't have asked you—"

"No, that's okay," I say quickly, worried that she might start crying again. "I can do that. I mean, if you really want me to..."

I'm actually thinking it's a little pathetic to send your friend to your ex to ask why he broke up with you. And what if he tells me something really embarrassing about her, like "she has really bad breath," or "she's boring," or "I hate the way she laughs"—what then? Do I come back and tell Nat the truth and make her feel even worse?

"You will?"

I nod. "Sure, if that's what you want."

"I do!"

"But that probably won't change anything, Nat." I want to warn her that it might even make it worse, but she seems so hopeful that I hate to be a wet blanket.

"I know. But maybe you can let him know how badly he's hurt me. I want him to know that I'm really hurting, Kim. I want him to feel guilty—for what he's done to me."

Okay, I'm not too sure about this. I mean, all he did was break up. Should he feel guilty about that? Maybe that's what Caitlin (Ben's sister) was trying to get across to us at snow camp—that one of the perils of dating is getting hurt when it's time to break up. She should try talking to her own brother!

"I'll do my best," I assure Nat. "But I'm not sure when I'll see him."

"One more thing?"

"What?"

"Would you mind running me home? I really don't think I can be at school today. I'll just be crying all day, and it's so humiliating."

"Sure," I tell her. And I drive her home and get back to school in time to make it to my second class. I keep an eye out for Ben, but I suspect he's lying low, probably worried that Nat will hunt him down and demand an explanation. Finally, I see him in the parking lot at the end of the day.

"Hey, Ben!" I walk over to him.

"Hey," he says in a flat-sounding voice. "What's up?"

"That's what I'm supposed to ask you." I go and stand next to his car.

"Oh..."

"Sorry to be so intrusive, but Nat's really hurting, and she wanted me to ask you why you broke up. And if you're not comfortable telling me, that's okay. I can just tell her I tried."

He seems to consider this. "It was just all wrong. I mean, I really liked Nat in the beginning, and we had fun together. But I probably shouldn't have started going out with her so soon after Torrey and I broke up, you know what I mean?"

"Rebound romance?"

He nods. "Yeah, kind of like that."

"But you went with Nat for almost two months, Ben. Why didn't you break it off sooner?"

"I don't know..." He looks away now, and I can tell he's uncomfortable, and suddenly I remember the disturbing thing that Torrey told me on my birthday when Matthew took me snowboarding. But how do you mention something like this to a guy? Even so, I'm feeling seriously irritated right now. I'm thinking, what if Ben put pressure on Nat, and when she refused, he decided she wasn't fun anymore? Now he's probably just looking for some other girl—one who will put out. It makes me sick!

"I'd been meaning to break up with her for weeks now," he finally says. "I guess I just didn't want to hurt her, you know?"

"So let me get this straight," I say in a firm but controlled voice. "The reason you broke up with Nat was because it was a rebound romance that never should've happened?"

"Pretty much."

"And that's it?" I stare at him now, pretending that I can see right through this little charade, hoping he'll just fess up and get it over with.

"Yeah, mostly."

"Mostly?" I wait.

"Okay, I knew God was telling me it was wrong, Kim. That was the final straw. I knew I'd be disobeying

God if I kept going with her. Do you get that?"

"And that's all?" I am really staring at him now, hoping that I'm making him really uncomfortable, because I just know there is more to this story. I just know that Mr. Perfect Benjamin O'Conner broke up with Natalie because she wouldn't "put out." And it's making me really, really angry!

"That's pretty much it, Kim."

"Fine," I snap at him. "If you say so, Ben. I'll be sure to tell Nat."

"And tell her I'm sorry," he says as I start to leave.

"For what?" I turn and look at him with, I imagine, plumes of fire shooting out my nostrils since I'm so enraged that I think I could actually rip his head off.

"For hurting her," he says with his eyes looking down. "I really wish I'd broken it off a lot sooner. That's where I blew it."

"Yeah, you did blow it," I agree as I turn away. "You can say that again."

Okay, I have to admit that it makes me feel lousy to lose my cool like that. It's so unlike me and actually quite uncomfortable. But it just really irks me to know that Ben was playing fast and loose with my best friend. Sure, maybe we weren't exactly acting like best friends at the time. But Nat and I go back—way back. And no one should get away with hurting her like that! I am so angry at Ben I could throw something—like him!

I'm still seething as I explain what happened to

Matthew, and while he attempts to be comforting, he doesn't really seem to get it. Then I go straight home and to my room. I know I should call Natalie and get this messy Ben business over with, but I'm still too angry to really talk about it, and I don't want to make her feel worse.

Then when I do call, her line is busy, and I imagine it's Ben calling to say he's sorry, and I'm imagining that they're having a nice long talk, and he's apologizing and trying to patch things up. Yeah, right.

Anyway, giving myself a little cool off time, I decide to answer a Just Jamie letter. And I pick one that could've been written by Ben. Maybe it was!

Dear Jamie,

I've been going with this girl for a while now, and I think I've shown her that I really care about her and that she can trust me and stuff. But she still doesn't want to have sex. Now I realize this is her choice, and I'm not going to force anything on her, but I'm thinking I should break up and find someone who understands me and my needs better. The problem is, I don't want to hurt her. Can you tell me the best way for a guy to break up?

Moving On

Oh, man, did this guy pick a good day to ask me this!

Dear Moving On,

You great big jerk! Any guy who dates a girl just to have sex should be whipped and beaten and hung out to dry! You are a totally insensitive moron, and I hope this poor girl figures it out and breaks up with you first!

Just Jamie!

Okay, I'll have to delete that response and try again later—sometime when I'm calmer and more rational. But I will answer the jerk's letter. You can count on that!

Sixteen

Monday, April 10

(A long day continues...)

It's after four when I try Nat's phone again, and this time she picks up. "How you doing?" I ask in what I hope is a more sympathetic tone than what I used with her earlier today.

"I've been better."

"I know..."

"Did you talk to him?"

"Yeah..."

"Want to come over here and tell me about it?" she says a little too eagerly, like she thinks it might be good news. "I'm babysitting."

So I go over, and Nat and I go to her room since Krissy and Micah look fairly occupied with cartoons, at least for the time being. And I tell her pretty much how the conversation with Ben went. And I even manage

NOT to editorialize it. Just give her the facts, I tell myself, and get it over with. Short and sweet.

"He was really sorry?" she says with what sounds like too much hope.

"Yeah, but mostly for the rebound romance part. He says he should've broken up with you when he figured that out."

"Oh..." Now she looks more hurt than ever.

"If it makes you feel any better, I really wanted to smack him."

"You did?" She looks surprised.

"Yeah. I think he was a jerk." I instantly regret that last comment. Too much said.

"Why do you think he was a jerk?"

I consider this. "Well, you know, for not breaking it off sooner, Nat. He should've known you were more into him than he was into you, and that you'd get hurt eventually."

"Oh...yeah."

"I'm sorry."

"Did he say anything else?" She looks slightly worried now. And I wonder if she suspects that he told me about pressuring her for sex, the same way he pressured Torrey. Like what guy would admit something like that to a girl? Well, other than the jerk who wrote Jamie, but that was anonymous.

"Not really," I tell her, and she looks relieved.

Then we hear Krissy and Micah getting into a squabble, and I tell Nat that I should go check on Mom.

"She was taking a nap when I got home," I say as we go downstairs, "but she's probably up by now."

"Thanks," Nat says in a sad voice.

"Hope you start feeling better soon."

"Yeah, me too."

Mom is up and puttering around in the kitchen when I get home. I fill her in a little on Natalie's broken heart. "Poor Natalie," she says as she pours herself a cup of green tea. "She's been through a lot."

"I know."

She sits down with her tea. "I'm so glad you girls are friends again."

"Me too."

"She'll probably need you more than ever right now."

"I guess."

It's about seven o'clock when Natalie calls me, and to my dismay, she sounds just as upset and hurt as before. Maybe even more so. "I really need to talk."

"Sure, go ahead."

"Can I come over?"

"Of course."

Soon we are both sitting on my bed, and I can tell that Natalie has something important to tell me. I'm certain it's about Ben, and I think I know what it is.

"I know I can totally trust you with this, Kim." Her eyes are still red and swollen from crying. "And I have to talk to someone..."

"Sure, Nat." I suspect she's about to divulge the truth about Ben and how he's not really who he seems to be.

And I am fully prepared to tell her what Torrey confessed to me in the bathroom that day. And hopefully we can both thoroughly bash Ben and get this thing over with.

"It's about me and Ben," she begins, her eyes downcast, as if she's studying the hand-stitched blocks on my quilt. "You see, after we'd gone out for about a month or so, well, I could tell things were starting to cool down between us. But by then I really, really liked him, and I didn't want to lose him. I guess I was kind of desperate, you know?"

"I know." I try to imagine that I know.

"Well, I'd heard this rumor...that Ben had broken up with Torrey because she wouldn't have sex with him, you know?"

I nod. "Actually I heard the same rumor."

"You did?"

"Yeah, from Torrey."

Nat's eyes get angry now. "That liar!"

"Liar?"

"Yeah. The rumor wasn't true."

"Huh?" Now I'm feeling really confused. "What do you mean?"

"I mean it wasn't true. But I thought it was."

"Okay, let's get this clear, Nat. You just said you'd heard the very same rumor about Ben and Torrey, right?"

"Yeah, but it wasn't true. Torrey had started that rumor herself."

"Why?"

"She and Ben had had a big fight about something else, and she'd gotten so mad at him that she broke up. Apparently she was sorry afterward, and when he and I got together, she started that rumor—hoping that I would hear it and it would make me break up with Ben. Do you get it?"

I'm not so sure, but I nod as if I do. "Okay, so you heard that rumor about Ben, and you honestly believed it, but you kept going out with him?"

"I really, really liked him, Kim. I think I was in love with him. I think I still am."

"Oh…" This is making my head hurt. But I know I need to listen and be here for Natalie. "So?"

"So when things started cooling down between us…well, I was worried that I was losing him. And I'd just watched this movie—a pretty steamy movie, if you know what I mean. And I thought, maybe there's only one way to keep this guy—and if I do it, then maybe he'll be mine forever, we'll get married, and everything will be okay."

My brows go up. "You <u>didn't</u>?"

She nods then looks away. "I <u>did</u>."

"You had sex with him?" I say, trying to conceal my shock that Natalie (the one who's always preaching at me…) that she would actually do this—have sex.

"Yeah."

"Seriously?"

She nods, and a tear streaks down her cheek. "I thought it was the only way to keep him. I thought that if he broke up with Torrey—" Now she starts crying harder. "I know it was stupid. Totally stupid! I am so stupid."

I put my hand on her shoulder. I don't even know what to say.

"The thing is—" She gasps. "I had to talk him into it. He didn't even want to. I was the one pressuring him—and as it turned out, we both lost our virginity that night!"

I glance uncomfortably at my door, hoping that neither of my parents are listening or anywhere nearby right now. Not that they're into eavesdropping. "Oh, Nat. I had no idea."

She's really sobbing now, and all I can do is hug her and tell her it's going to be okay. But what I'm thinking is, this is really, really sad. I mean, when I think about how Nat was nagging and warning me to be careful with Matthew all that time, and she's the one who gave in to temptation. Not only that, but she's partially responsible for Ben giving in too. It's just too much. I can't even wrap my mind around it.

"And–and," she sobs, still not ready to end her woeful tale, "it wasn't even fun! Not for either of us. It was just clumsy and messy and kinda gross. And after that night, things just kept getting worse between us. Oh, we had some great make-out sessions, and we actually tried it a couple more times, and I kept telling myself that this would change everything and that it would bind us together—that we'd really be one and get married and everything. But the truth is, I think it was what eventually drove us apart."

"Oh, Nat."

"But you know the worst part, Kim?"

I just shake my head. I can't even imagine.

"I can't pray now. I can't talk to God anymore."

"But He forgives you, Nat. You know that."

"I might know that in my head, but the rest of me isn't convinced. I feel like such a loser, such a hypocrite. I mean, I'm the one who kept telling you to be careful—" She lets out a choked sounding sob. "And I'm the one—the one who messed up."

"But you're sorry," I remind her. "God knows that, Natalie. You need to talk to Him. Just confess everything and ask Him to forgive you. You know that He will always forgive you. You've told me that very thing lots of times. But you need to go to Him and clean the slate."

"I know."

"And the sooner the better, Nat. Don't let it just pile up on you."

She nods. "Okay."

"And things will start getting better for you after you come clean with God. I'm sure you've learned a lot from this, and you're sure not going to make this same mistake again, right?"

She takes in a deep breath then slowly exhales. "I sure hope not."

Then I hug her again. "It's going to be okay, Nat."

She nods and then stands up. "I should go."

"Be sure and take care of this," I remind her as I walk her to the door. "Don't put it off, okay?"

"Yeah. Thanks, Kim."

Then she leaves, and I just stand and watch as she walks toward her house. There is absolutely no spring in her step, and in some ways she reminds me of a ghost—the ghost of Natalie McCabe.

"Everything okay?"

I kind of shake my head, suppressing tears. "Not exactly, Dad. Nat's having some, uh, personal problems."

"Oh."

I sense by his expression that he has no desire to hear about it. I know his job's been stressful lately, and that combined with worrying about Mom, well, it's like I can see him aging right before my eyes. In fact, I'm sure he has way more gray hair than he had last fall.

"But she'll be okay," I tell him quickly. "You know what they say, Dad. Time heals all wounds."

"Or wounds all heels."

I kind of laugh. "Yeah, that too."

Then he hugs me. "You're a good girl, Kim."

"Thanks, Dad."

As comforting as my dad's hug is, I feel even worse for Nat as I go back to my room. If her dad hadn't left them like that, cutting out on them when they really needed him, maybe things would've gone differently for Nat.

But then who knows? I do take time to pray for her

when I'm in my room. I even spend about an hour going over my prayer list before I go back and write my response to the "jerk" guy who wrote the letter about dumping his girlfriend without hurting her—yeah, right. Just the same, I suppose it helps me to cut him some grace after hearing about Ben. I can't believe that Ben's the one who got pressured into having sex for the first time. So weird. It's no wonder he feels so badly about the whole thing. Not that it makes him innocent—no way—but it does cast a totally different kind of light on everything.

Dear Moving On,

You say you've shown your girlfriend that you "really care about her" and that she can "trust" you, and yet it seems all you're really interested in is sex. Why not just be honest with her about this and see how she reacts. It's entirely possible that she'll want to break up with you, and you won't have to concern yourself with the "best way to break up." Especially because there really is no "best way." And speaking from experience, most girls want to be appreciated as more than just a sex object. But if that's what you're looking for, it sounds like you'll just have to keep looking.

Just Jamie

Seventeen

Saturday, April 15

I've never seen Natalie so down before. Not even when her dad left, and she was pretty devastated by that. When I see her at school, she reminds me of the walking dead, like a shadow of herself skulking down the halls. I try to spend as much time with her as I can, but even then she hardly talks to me, and by the end of the week, I felt like she was actually avoiding me. It's like she doesn't want to feel better. Or maybe she just can't. On Thursday, I asked her if she'd talked to God about this whole thing yet.

"Please don't preach at me, Kim," she said in a flat voice, ironic coming from the girl who's preached at me for years. But since I do remember what it feels like to be preached at, I am trying not to do this. Still, I'm worried about her.

"What's up with Ghost Girl today?" Matthew asked

me this afternoon. He started calling her Ghost Girl the other day when she wouldn't even speak to him. And I must admit the name is fitting with her pale blond hair just hanging around her paler-than-usual face (since she's not using any makeup these days), and then she's been constantly wearing this gray hoodie sweatshirt. It's really kind of eerie.

"She's not really talking to me either," I told him. "I don't know why she can't get over it." Of course, I haven't told Matthew the details of how Nat talked Ben into having sex and how she's beating herself up about it now. Somehow it just doesn't seem right.

"Give her time. Maybe another week...and I'll bet she'll pop out of it. Maybe she'll even pray for another boyfriend."

I frowned. "Don't make fun of her, Matthew."

"I'm not. I'm serious. My guess is that Nat is the kind of person who will pop back."

"Normally, I'd agree with you. I mean, I've seen her pop back from a lot of hard stuff. She's usually the perennial optimist who's getting on my case trying to get me to see the brighter side—a real Pollyanna."

He gave me a sideways hug. "Hey, I like that you're a realist."

"A realist with faith," I reminded him.

Then he asked how my mom was doing, and I felt my faith taking a nosedive. "Not so good. She seems to really be slowing down."

He frowned. "Bummer." Then he looked at me with

the most sincere expression. "You know I almost wish I was a Christian so I could pray for her too."

"Really?"

"Yeah. I mean, she's the sweetest lady I know, and it's like there's nothing anyone can really do for her..."

"Besides pray?"

He shrugged. "I guess it kind of feels like that."

"No one's stopping you from coming to God, Matthew."

"No one but me, you mean. But I couldn't fake it, Kim. If I ever take the big step—and I'm not saying I will—but it will be my way or no way."

"That's the only way to do it."

And as much as I'd like Matthew to have a relationship with God, it's gotten fairly low on my priority list. Not that I don't pray for him; I do. But with Nat's new zombie act and my mom looking sicker than ever, well, there's just a lot weighing me down right now. As a result, I told Matthew that I couldn't go out with him last night. Instead I stayed home and intentionally spent some time with my parents.

"Why aren't you going out tonight?" my mom asks as she watches me cleaning up the kitchen after dinner.

"I didn't want to." I put the last glass in the dishwasher.

"How about a comedy tonight?" Dad asks as he comes in holding two videos in his hands. His new theory is that laughter is very healing. And maybe it is. "'Groundhog Day' or 'The Great Outdoors'?"

"Thanks, honey, but not tonight," my mom says, slowly standing. "I don't think I can stay awake that long."

I don't mention the fact that it's not even seven yet. "Want some ginger tea, Mom?" Her stomach has really been bothering her, and ginger tea seems to soothe it a little.

"Sure. I'm going into the living room to put my feet up for a while."

So I make a pot of tea, then go in there to join her. Her head is leaning back against a pillow, her eyes are closed, and for a moment I think she's asleep.

"Oh, thanks, sweetheart," she says when she realizes I'm there. "Are you going to have some with me?"

"Sure." So I pour us both a cup of tea and sit down.

"I've been thinking about something lately," she says after a slow first sip. "Something that you might be able to help me with."

"Really? What is it?"

"Well, I've told you about my younger sister before..."

"The one who left home when she was seventeen, and you never heard from since?"

Mom nods. "Shannon."

"Wasn't it after your mom died that she left?" I say, trying to remember how the story went since it's been a few years since I heard it.

"Yes, Shannon was a senior in high school...I was just finishing college...and, well, our dad wasn't handling our mother's death too well...it was hard on Shannon."

"And she just took off."

"That's right. She called me a few times during that first year, mostly for money, but then we lost touch and I never heard from her since."

"And you're thinking about her now?"

"I wonder if...how she's doing...if she's okay...you know our mother died of ovarian cancer...and it's genetic and..."

"You wonder if Shannon has had it too?"

"I do."

"But what does this have to do with me, Mom?"

"Well, I know how good you are at searching up things on your computer, and I wondered if..."

"If I could locate Shannon?"

She makes a sad half smile. "Do you think it's even possible, Kim?"

"I do. But you'll have to give me as much information as you've got on her. I mean, I know your maiden name was Busche, and that's not terribly common, at least with that spelling. That will help, but do you have anything else on her? Like a social security number?"

"I don't have a social security number, but I do have a box with some memorabilia." She takes a last sip of tea and sets her cup down. "It's in my room."

So I help her up and slowly walk with her to her bedroom. When we get to her room, she is so tired that she needs to sit down. I help to ease her into the armchair by the bed, then get her comfy blanket and lay it on her lap. "Okay?" I ask, feeling uncertain because she seems to be breathing so heavily.

She nods. "Not very strong these days..."

I sit on the bed and wait for her to catch her breath. I wish there was something I could say or do that would change this. I wish I could share some of my energy and health with her. Instead I just look at my hands in my lap, and I pray. I silently beg God to heal her. "Do it now!" I am shouting in my head. "Please, heal her right now, God! I'm begging You, asking You, please, do a miracle! Please, please, please!"

"The box is in the bottom right-hand drawer of my bureau," she finally says, jerking me back to reality.

"Oh." I go over, pull open the drawer, take out a pale blue cloth-covered box, and bring it over to her. Then I sit and watch as she slowly unties the faded ribbon that holds it closed and then removes the lid. There's not much in the box: papers, some photos, a yearbook. Mom picks up a photo and holds it up for me to see. It's a teenaged girl with long dark brown hair. She's wearing a fringed leather vest, wild-colored flared pants that are straight from the sixties, and a big smile.

"She was really pretty," I say as I look at her even features and big brown eyes. "Kind of reminds me of Julia Roberts, well, when she was younger."

"Yes." Mom hands me another photo. "She was very pretty. And that wasn't even a great picture of her."

I take the second photo, a head and shoulders shot

that looks like it must've been taken for school. "Wow, she was beautiful."

"Shannon was a free spirit." Mom leans back in her chair, looking at another picture with two girls this time. I can tell that one of the girls is Shannon. She has on a very short orange and hot-pink dress and white knee-high boots. The other one I suspect is Mom.

"Is that you?" I point to the serious-looking college-aged girl wearing a somber gray jumper over a neat white blouse.

"Yes. It was shortly before Mother died."

"Oh..."

"Shannon and father argued a lot," Mom continues. "Over her clothes and appearance and the boys she dated and staying out late. I think all the fighting just made it easier for her to leave after Mother died."

"That's too bad."

"Shannon was certain that she was going to make it big in Hollywood."

I study the pretty, bright-eyed girl and think perhaps she might've had a real chance. "Did she?"

"Not that we ever heard."

"Oh."

"I just wonder what became of her, Kim. Do you think you can find out?"

"I'll do my best."

"What's going on here?" my dad says as he peeks his head into the bedroom. "You girls taking some kind of sentimental journey? No guys allowed?"

Mom laughs. "Of course you're allowed, Allen. I was just showing Kim some pictures of Shannon."

"I see."

"Did you ever meet her, Dad?"

He shakes his head and comes over to look. "No. But your mom's told me a little about her."

"I've asked Kim to see if she can find Shannon on her computer. I know it's a long shot, but I'm just curious. I wonder what's become of her...if she's still around."

Dad puts a hand on Mom's shoulder. "Well, if anyone can find her, I'm sure Kim's your girl."

Mom smiles. "Kim's my girl whether or not she finds her."

"Do you mind if I get started?" I say. "I'm pretty curious."

"Please, do," says Mom. "I'm curious too."

So I begin my search tonight. But after trying several things, getting a couple of false starts and a few disappointments, I finally give up. Just for the night. I will continue my search tomorrow. Then I take a few minutes to e-mail both Matthew and Natalie before I force myself to answer some Just Jamie letters. And if you ask me, the first one I read is totally whacked.

Dear Jamie,

I'm fifteen, but everyone says I'm mature for my age, plus I look older. I can easily pass for eighteen. Also most of my friends are older than me. Here's my problem. I really like "Tom" (my soccer coach), and he really likes me. I babysit his two little boys quite a lot—I adore them and they totally love me—and when Tom takes me home afterward, we always have these really great discussions, and he treats me like I'm an adult. Lately he's started kissing me good night—on the lips. The problem is that Tom is still married to his wife. He says he's definitely going to leave her, but that she's going through some hard stuff, and he doesn't want to make things worse. See, that's how thoughtful he is. Anyway, I'm afraid to tell anyone about our relationship because I know they won't understand. But Tom and I are really in love, and I'm certain that someday he will marry me. But what should I do in the meantime?

15 going on 30

Dear 15,

A married man (with children!) has no business getting romantically involved with a fifteen-year-old girl. And any smart fifteen-year-old girl should keep a safe distance from him. "Tom" is putting you (as well as himself) in an extremely dangerous position. You need to cut off your relationship with him immediately. If he gets any more involved with you, he is at risk of being arrested for serious charges like child molestation or child abuse or statutory rape. You say you are "mature," and if that's true, you need to make the mature decision to get out of this situation ASAP. Otherwise you could be seeing Tom arrested, charged, convicted, serving time while his wife and children suffer for his poor choices at home. Do you really want to have any part in something like that?

Just Jamie

Okay, I was probably a little harsh. But I want this girl to get the point. And maybe that stupid "Tom" will read my column and get a clue too. What on earth makes some people think that crud like that is acceptable? I mean, I've seen this stuff in the news, but you like to think it happens someplace else, not your hometown.

Eighteen

Thursday, April 20

I feel like darkness is closing in on me. Not to sound overly dramatic, but the pressure is intense. First of all, Natalie is not getting over the Ben thing. She's more depressed than ever. Even her mom is concerned. She called me from work yesterday and asked if I knew what was wrong.

"Natalie won't talk to me," she told me.

"Join the club," I said. Probably not encouraging, but I feel like I'm hitting my head against the wall trying to get through to Nat these days. I'm ready to give up.

"What do you think I should I do?" she asked, desperation clear in her voice. And I realized here is a hard-working single mom trying to raise two young kids and a teenager with a broken heart. Not easy.

"I don't really know, Mrs. McCabe," I said helplessly. "I'm kind of at a loss with her myself."

She sighed. "Well, maybe she'll snap out of it. But if you think of anything, will you let me know? Call me at work if you need to." Then she gave me the number and hung up.

But when I sat down at my computer, I began to think about it. Why didn't I have any good advice? What would Jamie say? That's when I decided to Just Ask.

Dear Jamie,

My best friend recently got her heart broken after having sex (which really compromised her values) with her boyfriend who later broke up with her. She's so bummed that she won't talk to anyone, and she can't seem to get over it. She just walks around with a cloud hanging over her, not interested in anything. What should I do?

KP

Dear KP,

It sounds like your friend is depressed. Maybe it would help her to talk to a counselor or pastor. As her best friend you should recommend this. If she refuses, try talking to her parent(s) about getting some kind of professional counseling.

Just Jamie

Okay, I don't plan on actually running this letter, but it did seem an obvious answer when I actually sat down and wrote it all out. I'm starting to wonder if Jamie is my alter ego or something—like she pops in when I sit down to write and just takes over for me. Anyway, it seemed like good advice (if I do say so myself), and I thought it was worth a try. So I called Nat, and in the nicest way possible I attempted to tell her that I thought she needed help.

"Help for what?" she said in that dead-sounding flat voice.

"To get over this thing with Ben."

"I'm over it."

"No, you're not, Nat. Everyone around you can see that you're not. You're hurting, and I think you've actually become depressed. You need help."

"Like my mom can afford that."

"What about a counselor at your church, wouldn't that be—?"

"No way."

"But you need help, Nat. I'm worried about you. Your mom's even worried."

"I'm fine," she said with a note of finality.

"But, Nat—"

"I gotta go."

So later on I called her mom at work and told her my idea about counseling. "I suggested this to Nat, but she wasn't interested."

"Counseling?"

"Yeah, without telling you too much—for Nat's sake—I will say that I know some details of her breakup with Ben that I think could be really disturbing to her.

She talked to me about it, but she needs to talk to a real professional, you know? Are there counselors at your church?"

"Sure. My friend Marge is a really good counselor. In fact, she's suggested that Natalie come in sometime. She was worried that the divorce might be hard on her."

"Why don't you encourage Nat to go then?"

"Maybe I will. I guess I just didn't realize that whatever she's going through would derail her like this. I mean, she's been such a trooper through everything."

"I guess we all have our limits."

"I guess so."

And I feel like I'm getting close to my limit too. Besides Nat, it seems as if my mom is getting worse. And while I keep praying and trying to have faith, I am really scared that she's not going to make it. I can't imagine life without my mom. It's like I don't even want to think about it. And I don't really want to talk about it either. And I'm pretty sure that my dad doesn't want to talk about it. So we just keep tiptoeing around, acting like she's got a bad case of the flu that will go away soon.

And it's times like these when I think it might help if my boyfriend were a Christian—someone who could encourage me through this darkness. Not only does Matthew not have any answers, all he brings up are more questions. And I know he doesn't get faith at all. I guess I miss Nat's encouragement not to give up. I doubt that she's even praying at all these days, much less for my mom. It's like we've all fallen into a dark hole.

But then there's my mom. Considering the pain that I know she's in, she's amazingly cheerful. I guess that's one reason Dad and I keep deceiving ourselves that she's going to get better. And maybe she is. Maybe God is just testing our faith right now. Does He do that? Oh, maybe I'm the one who needs counseling. I don't know. Maybe I should ask the expert.

Dear Jamie,

My mother has stage four ovarian cancer. I've been believing that she's going to get better—that God is going to heal her—but I'm just not sure. My doubts seem to be growing with each day. Also I have a friend who may be clinically depressed, my boyfriend isn't a Christian, and I feel like I need some encouragement or insight or something. What should I do?

KP

Dear KP,

Stage four ovarian cancer is very serious. If you've done any research, you probably know that it's almost always terminal. It sounds like you need to talk to someone about this and the other things that are troubling you. Why not make an appointment with a professional who can give you a handle on all the stuff you're going through?

Just Jamie

Sure, let's just send everyone to the shrink, Jamie. You got any other great answers? Okay, maybe it's true; maybe I do need help. But I haven't the slightest idea of where to go. I mean, Faith Fellowship is a pretty small church, and besides the pastors we don't have any professional counselors there. I suppose I could talk to a pastor, but what would I say? And what would he say to me? "Trust God, Kim, He knows what's best." Or would he tell me to "Just pray harder," like Nat has done in the past.

Finally, I decide to quit second-guessing everyone, and I call up the church. I'm pretty sure there's nothing they can do to help, but I end up with Pastor Tony on the phone, and he makes an appointment with me for after school tomorrow. Now I'm feeling kind of freaked. Like what am I going to say to him? I think I've actually talked to him about three times so far. But here's one good thought: At least I can tell Nat that I'm going in for counseling. Maybe that will make her see her own need.

Friday, April 21

As I go into the church and inform the secretary that I'm here for my appointment with Pastor Tony, I tell myself it's no big deal. People do this every day. Just relax, Kim, Tony's a really nice guy and an intelligent pastor. What can go wrong?

But my palms are cold and sweaty, and my voice comes out in a scratchy croak when I merely attempt to say, "Hello."

"Have a seat, Kim," he says in a kind voice. "I'm so glad you came in to talk. I've actually been meaning to give you a call."

"Me?" I sit in the chair across from him and study his desk. There are a few papers here and there, but all in all it's fairly neat. And there are photos of his wife and little boys, and not for the first time I think what an attractive family they are.

"Yes." Pastor Tony leans forward, elbows on his desk, and looks evenly at me. "How's your mom doing?"

That's when I totally lose it. I start just sobbing and crying, and Pastor Tony moves his chair around to the other side of the desk, and the secretary, just outside the door, comes in with a box of tissues and starts patting my back. And without me saying a word, the two of them each put a hand on my shoulder, and they start to pray. At first I am a little alarmed. I mean, no one has ever done this for me before. But then I begin to relax, and although it's hard to focus completely, I pick up bits and pieces of what they are praying.

"Give her strength, dear Lord..."

"And give her the peace that passes understanding..."

"Hold her in Your arms, Father God..."

"Please, bind their family together in Your never-ending love..."

"Let Kim bring all her questions and doubts to You..."

After a few minutes they are both saying, "Amen." And feeling self-conscious although somewhat better, I thank them and wonder if that was it? Is my session over now?

But Tony sits back down in his chair. "You've got a heavy load to carry, Kim. But God doesn't expect you to carry it alone. He wants you to bring all your worries and fears to Him, and if you get too tired to carry them to God, He wants you to trust your Christian brothers and sisters to carry them to God for you. That's how we bear one another's burdens. It's like we carry them to God and place them at His feet. Sometimes we do it on our own, and sometimes we ask others for help. Does that make sense?"

I nod without saying anything.

"Want to talk about how you're feeling about your mom now?"

I nod again then clear my throat. "I think my mom is going to die," I confess for probably the first time ever.

He nods. "We're all going to die, Kim."

"I know. But I had been trying to believe that my mom was going to beat the cancer, that God was going to heal her, and now I don't think I believe it anymore."

"How does that make you feel toward God?"

Now I really consider this. And regardless of whether or not I'm talking to a pastor, I want to be honest. "I guess it makes me kind of mad."

"I can understand that."

"I mean, my mom is one of the sweetest, kindest,

most humble—" I start crying again.

"And you wonder why God would allow such a saintly woman to die so young?"

I sniff. "Yeah, I guess I do."

"You're not alone, Kim. I think most of us question God's choices at some time in life."

"Even you?"

"I'm sure you've heard about my brother."

I blink. "Oh, yeah. I mean, I've heard about Clay and the school shooting. I guess I almost forgot that he was your brother. That must've been painful."

"It was. Clay was such a cool kid. He'd gone through some hard stuff and then really turned his life around. I don't know if I've ever known anyone with such a heart for God."

"Yeah, I've heard that."

"And even though I was a pastor, I had moments when I questioned God, and I got angry too."

"How did you get over it?"

"Well, I guess it helped when I allowed myself to question God. I mean, at least it kept the communication doors open. But that's when I first began to realize that there's so much that I'll never really understand about God and life and death—and that I'll just have to trust Him for a lot of things until I get to heaven. And I've learned there's great freedom and release in accepting that."

"Instead of asking why, why, why all the time?"

"It's not that God is intimidated by our why

questions, but I think He wants us to grow up and go to the next step, and that's to say, 'God, I don't know why, I may never know why, but I still love You, I still trust You.' You know what I mean?"

"Kind of. But I don't think I'm there yet."

He sort of laughs. "I don't think any of us really are. I got a flat tire this morning, which made me late to an important meeting, and I felt myself asking why God? in a very impatient way to be perfectly honest."

"Did you ever figure out why?"

He laughs louder now. "Not really. Oh, I'm sure I could use some more lessons in patience, and I think it was good for that. But sometimes things happen where it's hard to see the reasoning. Like last year's tsunami in Asia. I'm sure all of us were asking why. But it didn't really change anything. And although we heard some miraculous stories, there were still lots and lots of unexplainable tragedies."

"And I was one of the ones who kept wondering why."

"You're in good company. But here's what I think, Kim. I think that God can use these tragedies to remind us that our lives here on earth are limited. We can't live in our physical bodies forever. And yet our American culture gets consumed with the here and now sometimes; people spend big bucks trying to stay young and healthy, like they think they're going to be walking around in these earth suits forever. But that's not the case—not for anyone. I think God just wants us to realize that physical death isn't really the end—it's just the beginning of the second part, the exciting part that will go on for eternity. Do you get that?"

"I guess I do. Or sort of. Maybe the problem is how much I think I'm going to miss her."

"Of course you will. But that's only because you love her so much, and because she loves you. What if you didn't miss her?"

"That'd be pretty sad."

"Now, I don't want to make light of this, Kim, because accepting the death of a loved one is probably the hardest thing we ever do. But God can and will get you through it—if you bring it to Him. And if you can't bring it yourself, ask your Christian family to help you. Can you do that?"

"I think so."

Then we talk about the stages of grief, and he gives me a little book to read and tells me that my dad may need to talk to someone too. "I'm available," he says.

"He might want someone from where my parents go to church."

"So they are believers then?"

I nod.

"Well, that answers my last question."

"My mom's faith is a lot stronger than my dad's, but I know he's a Christian, deep down. Just a quiet one, you know."

He smiles. "Nothing wrong with that."

Then I thank him, and he makes me promise to

come back and see him anytime I need to talk, and I promise that I will. And I'm pretty sure that I will. I think Pastor Tony is a very wise pastor, and it makes me feel better knowing that he's lost a close loved one too.

I call Nat after I get home and tell her that I just got done with my first counseling session.

"Did you tell my mom I need counseling?" she demands.

"Sort of. But she asked my opinion, Nat, and I think you do."

"Thanks a lot." Long silence. "What else did you tell her?"

"Nothing," I say quickly. "I just said I thought you needed to talk to someone."

"Well, now I'm supposed to go see Marge tomorrow."

"Hey, if I can do it, you should be able to do it too."

"Maybe I will. Maybe I won't." Then she hangs up.

I stand there holding the receiver in disbelief. I don't think Nat's ever hung up on me before.

Then I go to my computer and check to see if I've gotten any e-mail. I've sent out a few posts trying to track down the mysterious Shannon Busche, but so far no leads. To my surprise there is an answer now. And as far as I can tell, it seems to be from Shannon herself. But I should probably check this out a little more before I tell Mom and get her hopes up. It could be someone just pulling my leg or looking for free handouts.

Dear Kim,

My maiden name was Shannon Busche, and I had a sister named Patricia, who was five years older than me. Who are you, and why are you looking for me?

Shannon

Okay, so far this is only the same information that I sent out in my own e-mail. I need more confirmation than this.

Dear Shannon,

I really hope that you're the right person. I am Patricia's daughter, and she recently asked me to search for you. Can you tell me a little bit more about yourself to confirm that it's really you? 1) What are your parents' first names? 2) What is my mom's middle name? 3) Where and when were you born? I hope you don't mind. I only want to confirm that you are really my mom's sister. She has some health problems, and I don't want to get her hopes up unless it's the real thing. I'm sure you'll understand.

Sincerely, Kim

Nineteen

Monday, April 24

My mom had to go into the hospital last night. She was having trouble breathing, and the ambulance came for her. I've never been so scared in my life. Dad and I followed in his car, and by the time we got to ER, Mom had been stabilized with oxygen. Even so, they wanted to keep her overnight. So Dad and I both stayed overnight as well. We took turns sleeping on the couch in Mom's room and the couch out in the "family room," which is a waiting room with furniture, a TV, a microwave, and stuff to make the families of patients feel more at home. Yeah, right. But at least the couch wasn't too lumpy.

"Kim," my mom said early this morning when I went in to check on her. "Isn't it Monday? You should go to school, sweetheart."

"It's okay, Mom. I'd rather be here with you. Besides,

you know that my grades are up, and it won't hurt to miss a day."

She smiled. "I know that. But I want you to keep them up. Besides, I'm going to be released later this morning. Why don't you have Dad take you home so you can go to school?"

"Why don't you just take my car." Dad held out his keys. "I'll call a taxi when your mom gets released."

There seemed to be no point in arguing, and relieved that Mom was doing better and about to be released, I decided it might be less stressful for them if I just went to school. After a quick shower and change of clothes, I even got there in time for second period. And although I tried to focus on my classes, I felt like I was just going through the paces, like my brain wasn't really engaged.

"You okay?" Matthew asked when he met me, as usual, at my locker before lunch.

So I told him about Mom and the hospital, and despite my resolve to be strong, I started to cry. Matthew put his arms around me and just held me for a couple of minutes. And even though he's not a Christian and unable to pray, it was a comfort.

But later on I saw Natalie, and she must've observed our embrace. "Must be nice to have a guy to hug you," she said in a bitter tone.

I didn't bother to explain, but I did ask her about the counseling session.

"I didn't go. I'm fine."

Well, I just didn't have the emotional strength to go

there with her, so I just shrugged and said, "Whatever. It's your life, Nat."

"That's right. It is." Then she walked away.

Okay, I don't know why Nat's treating me like this. It's not as if I had anything to do with her and Ben. And the truth is, I don't really care right now. I mean, I love her, but I don't think I can help her. I can barely help myself.

By the time I get home, I'm exhausted but relieved to see both my parents are home. Mom is taking a nap in her bedroom, and Dad is working on his computer.

"Everything okay?" I ask him.

He looks up and nods. "Yeah. We have an oxygen tank now. In case she needs it."

"Oh..." I start to leave.

"Something else, Kim."

"Yeah?"

"The hospital has signed us up for hospice."

"Hospice?"

"It's a social service."

"Huh? What for?"

"For your mom."

"But what is it?"

"Hospice is for terminal patients."

I swallow now and just look at my dad. "Meaning?"

Dad's face kind of crumbles now, and he puts his head in his hands and leans forward on his desk. His pain is so obvious, so heavy, so hopeless that it's breaking my heart. I go over to him and put a hand on his shoulder.

We both cry for a while, then Dad hands me his big white handkerchief, and I dry my face and hand it back. He manages to find some dry spots on it to wipe his face then sighs. "I think we're going to lose her, Kim."

"I know, Dad."

"The doctor doesn't know how much time is left..."

I don't say anything.

"That's why they want us to have hospice."

"But what exactly is it, Dad? What does it mean?"

He hands me a pamphlet. "Trained nurses will come in and help care for your mom. She's been doing real well on her own, but she's so weak now... Even simple things like bathing are difficult for her."

"I could stay home and help her."

"I know, honey, but this is better. Your mom would feel terrible if you missed school to—"

"But it's okay—"

"I know you're willing, Kim. But this is better. They'll also provide counselors and whatever it takes to get through this. Your mom wants it too."

"Well, okay. I mean, I'm fine with that."

"I know this is hard for you."

"It's hard for you too, Dad." Then I remember last week's counseling session and tell him briefly about it.

"That was a smart thing to do, honey."

"Well, I had to write to Jamie first, to get some advice."

This makes him smile, then he reaches out and takes my hand and squeezes it. "I thank God for you."

"Same back at you, Dad."

"I have to finish up this paperwork now," he says apologetically.

"No problem. I'm going to take a nap anyway."

But instead of taking a nap I go online to check my e-mail. To my pleased surprise, I have a response from Shannon again, and she answers all my questions perfectly then asks what's wrong with my mom.

Dear Shannon,

My mom has stage four ovarian cancer. By the time she was diagnosed, it was pretty much untreatable. The doctor doesn't know how long she has to live. I know that your mother died from the same thing, and this might be hard for you to deal with, but I think it would mean a lot to my mom to talk to you. Do you think you'd be ready for a phone conversation anytime soon? I can set it up, and we can call you so you don't have to pay for the call. Let me know.

Sincerely, Kim

Wednesday, April 26

The hospice nurses are really nice, and I can see why my parents agreed to sign up for this service. And in some ways, things are feeling more hopeful at our house. Mom even seems to have more energy, but I suspect this is because she has a lot more help getting things done.

I probably didn't realize how much she still did to keep our household going. I mean, I know that I'm helping out a lot, but because of hospice we will also have a housekeeper coming in once a week now. Even so, I don't feel good about being gone from the house for long, and even when I'm in class, I keep my cell phone on, just to vibration mode and in my pocket, but I want to make sure that Dad can reach me if anything changes.

"Don't worry, honey," he assured me last night. "I think things are settling down. Having this help is making a difference in your mom's health. You don't need to be on needles and pins all the time."

"Maybe not. But I want to stick around. I was even thinking about canceling out on the prom—"

"No, Kim. Don't even think about that. It would hurt your mom so much to have you miss the prom. She's so excited about it and the dress and everything. You can't even consider canceling."

And so I promised I wouldn't and also that I wouldn't mention the idea to Mom since Dad was convinced it would trouble her. Even so, I will be taking my cell, and I'll ask Matthew to keep it in his pocket for me.

Then tonight when I'm checking e-mail, I see that Shannon has responded to my last post, and I can hardly read it fast enough. First she apologizes for not writing sooner, and then says she wants to talk to Mom and gives me her phone number. So I decide to call her.

"This is Kim Peterson," I tell the woman who

answers the phone. "I'm Patricia's daughter and I—"

"Oh, you must want my mom," she says quickly. And after a while another voice comes on.

"This is Shannon."

"Shannon, this is Kim, Patricia's daughter."

"Oh, Kim, is Patricia there? Can I talk to her?"

"Well, I wanted to talk to you first," I say nervously. "I mean, my mom is pretty sick, and I don't want her to get upset or anything."

"Does she even want to talk to me?"

"Oh, yes, she definitely does. But I haven't told her that I found you yet. I wanted to be sure."

"Oh, okay. What's the plan then?"

"I want to tell Mom that I found you, and then if it's okay, we'll call you back. Is this a good time?"

"Yeah, it's fine. I'll tell Maya to stay off the phone."

"Is that your daughter?"

"Yeah. On a good day."

I'm not sure how to respond. "Okay then, I'll talk to Mom and then we'll call."

"I'll be here."

So I find Dad and tell him my news. "Do you think it's too late to call tonight? I don't want to wear Mom out or anything."

"Let me see how she's feeling."

As it turns out, Mom is totally thrilled that I've found Shannon. "I want to talk to her. The sooner the better." Then she smiles. "I knew you could do it, sweetheart!"

So we get Mom comfortable in her chair by the bed,

bring in the phone, and with trembling fingers I dial.

"Do you want me to go?" I ask, uncertain.

"No, stay. Both of you stay."

So Dad and I both sit on the bed and wait until Mom says, "Hello, this is Patricia. Is this Shannon?" And then she starts crying. "Oh, it's so good to hear your voice again. How are you?" Long pause. "Oh, that's too bad." Another pause. "Oh, I'm doing okay. I've got some help in the house now, and I feel like I have a little more energy now."

Then Mom asks her about her life, her family, kids, where is she living, and then mostly just listens. I wish she was talking on a speaker phone because I'd like to hear the answers. Finally, we can tell that Mom's getting tired, and Dad gives her a signal to hang up.

"You can talk again tomorrow," he says quietly.

"Well, I guess I should go for now," Mom says in a weary voice. "But I'd love to talk to you again, Shannon. Can I call you tomorrow?" Pause. "Oh, I'd love to see you—and your daughter too—do you think it's really possible?" Another pause. "That would be wonderful, Shannon. Yes, we'll talk tomorrow. Take care, sweetheart. And just know that I love you. I've always loved you. Good-bye."

Mom is crying again when she hangs up and Dad helps her to lie down in bed. "You need to rest a little, Patty."

She leans back and closes her eyes without protesting.

"You can tell us about Shannon later." He pulls the blanket up over her. "After you've rested a little."

She sort of nods without talking, and Dad and I tiptoe from the room. I really want to hear more about this mysterious aunt, but I realize I'll have to be patient. And if what we heard Mom saying was true, maybe we'll even get to meet her.

I decide to distract myself with a letter for my column, but it takes a while before I find something that's a little bit light.

Dear Jamie,

I'm thirteen and I was really curious as to what it would feel like to kiss a guy on the mouth, but I think I'm too young to do that. So I decided to try kissing our cat on the mouth. Well, just as I was doing this my older brother walked into my bedroom and started laughing so hard I thought he was going to pass out. I begged him not to tell anyone, but he said he was going to tell everyone unless I did his chores that day. So I did, but then he said I had to do them the next day and the next. Now I think I'll be his slave forever. What should I do?

Cat Kisser

Dear Cat Kisser,

I seriously doubt that anyone would be too interested to hear that you kissed your cat. (Did he have fish breath?) I guess you need to ask yourself what's worse—allowing your brother to blackmail you into being his slave indefinitely or being embarrassed for about five seconds if he tells someone? I'm sure lots of people kiss their pets—get over it.

Just Jamie

Twenty

Thursday, April 27

Mom was up early this morning, sitting in the breakfast nook with a cup of tea. For a moment I almost thought that everything was back to normal, but then I noticed the dark hollow circles around her eyes.

"How are you doing?" I asked as I poured a glass of orange juice and waited for my bagel to pop up.

"Wonderful," she said with a smile.

I spread some cream cheese on my bagel then took my breakfast over to join her. "Are you going to talk to Shannon again today?"

She nodded. "Yes! I'm so happy that you found her, Kim. Thank you so much."

"Where does she live?"

"Beverly Hills."

"Beverly Hills? As in California?"

"Yes, isn't that something? She told me that she'd

been married to someone quite well-known, but that they'd divorced about ten years ago."

"Someone quite well-known?" Was it possible that my mystery aunt was someone famous? Or at least associated with someone famous? Interesting.

"She has a teenaged daughter, just a couple years younger than you, Kim. Her name is Maya, and it sounds like she's quite a handful."

"Yeah, she seemed to have an attitude when I talked to her."

"The good news is that Shannon wants to fly out with Maya to see us. We're going to try to nail it down today. Isn't this exciting?"

I nodded as I chewed a bite. "I can't wait to meet them."

As usual, I gave Nat a ride to school, and as usual she acted like Ghost Girl. Seriously, I'm not sure how much longer I can take this. When I asked her about counseling, she just ignored me. Finally I started up this monologue about locating Shannon, filling in the parts where Ghost Girl would respond if she was willing.

"She sounds really interesting," I say.

"How's that?" I ask for Ghost Girl.

"Well, for one thing she lives in Beverly Hills, and for another she was married to someone famous." I pause.

"Someone famous?" I ask with the kind of interest the old Nat would've shown.

"Yeah, but we don't know who yet." Another pause.

"Do you think he's a movie star?"

My turn. "The thought went through my head..." And on I go, amusing myself as I drive us to school. By the time we get there, I'm seriously wondering if Nat might need electroshock therapy before she goes into a complete comatose state.

"You need to snap out of this," I tell her as I lock my Jeep. "You're really starting to freak me."

"Sorry." But the tone of her voice doesn't really sound sorry. It sounds angry and frustrated and stuck. It's like she's trapped in this place, and she can't get out.

"I wish you'd go see Marge," I say as we go inside.

She says nothing, and I decide that for my own health's sake I better just let Nat deal with her own problems today. Although I do pull something sneaky.

We have this anonymous box in the counseling office where people can drop in notes of concern about themselves or someone else. Oh, I know a lot of kids make up stuff—either to be funny or to get someone in trouble—but I've heard that some serious notes are put in there as well. It was originally set up as a way to inform a counselor if someone was having suicidal thoughts or perhaps planning to bring an automatic weapon to school to wipe out a science class.

Anyway, I take a few minutes during first period to write an anonymous note about Natalie. I figure it can't hurt. I use my left hand to write it, and the handwriting doesn't look anything like mine.

> I'm worried about Natalie McCabe. She is extremely depressed and refuses to see a counselor. Natalie is usually very upbeat and positive, but she has been like this for at least two weeks, and I think she needs professional help.

Then right before lunchtime, I ask Matthew to drop it in the box for me, just in case Nat happens by.

"The deed is done," he tells me when we meet up again in the cafeteria. It's the first time I've really talked to him today, and I can't wait to tell him about my Aunt Shannon. I've already started calling her that. I hope she doesn't mind.

"That's very cool," he says as I hand him my chocolate pudding to finish off for me.

"Yeah, I can't wait to hear more about her. She and Mom are discussing travel plans today."

"How is your mom?"

Matthew already knows about hospice and everything. "She seems to have perked up," I tell him. "She was up early this morning, and I'm thinking this whole thing with her sister might help her to get better, or at least to hang on longer." As much as it hurts to say those words, I am trying to get myself to a place where I'm not fooling myself anymore.

"So you've given up on the miracle?"

"No," I say quickly. "I'm still praying, and I know that God could heal her. I'm just not certain that He will. I mean, God lets people die every day. It's not like you can exactly hold Him back, you know. It's more about trusting Him, about believing that He's got this all figured out and has a reason for His timing."

Matthew really seems to consider this. "I guess that makes sense."

"Seriously?"

He nods. "Yeah, more sense than some of the stuff I've heard."

"Wow."

"So, you all ready for the big night?"

I grin at him. "I think so." He still hasn't told me much about "his plan" for the evening—just that it'll be special and that I won't be disappointed. "It doesn't involve a stretch limo and a bunch of alkies, does it?" I asked last week, and he just laughed. "Not this time." I'm also sure that it doesn't involve a "group" date like I suggested a few weeks ago.

Of course, he reminded me that our "group" date at the Harvest Dance didn't really work out too well. Besides, neither Cesar or Jake are going to the prom, although Marissa is going with Robert. And while I told her it'd be fun to see her there, I had absolutely no desire to "double" with those two. I've also heard that they've booked a hotel room afterward. Well, that's their choice—not mine. And thankfully I'm certain that Matthew has no such plans.

I also heard another rumor today, one I seriously hope Nat hasn't gotten wind of since I'm sure it would push her right over the edge: Torrey and Ben have "secretly" gotten back together, and they are "secretly" going to the prom. Marissa told me this little news flash in art. How she heard about it is a mystery, but I have a feeling she could be right. Just the same, these lips are sealed.

Friday, April 28

"It's all settled," Mom tells me after school today. "Shannon got a great deal on airline tickets—she used one of those websites where you make an offer, and she just called to tell me it was accepted. She and Maya will be here on Monday."

"Monday! That's fantastic, Mom. But doesn't Maya have school?"

"Maya is home-schooled," Mom informs me.

"That's cool."

"So, do you have everything ready for the big night?"

"I think so."

"Maybe not everything..." she says mysteriously.

"Huh?"

Then she pulls out an envelope and hands it to me. I can tell that it's from a beauty salon downtown. "What's this?"

"A certificate and an appointment. I had Julie, the hospice worker, pick it up for me today. I thought you could get your hair and nails done tomorrow. Actually it was her idea, but I think it's a good one."

"Oh, Mom!" I throw my arms around her. "This is so

awesome. Thanks. I was just going to do my hair myself, but this is way better."

"The appointment is for ten in the morning," she tells me. "And I hope you don't mind that I made an appointment for myself too."

"That is so cool, Mom. What are you going to have done?"

"It's been quite a while since I've had my hair cut, and I don't want to look like an old frump when Shannon gets here—she was always so fashionable. And I thought I might even get my nails done too." She laughs now. "Just for fun."

I hug her again. "That is way cool, Mom. I can't wait!"

And so I'm feeling really hopeful about Mom now. It's like this thing with Shannon coming to visit really has given her a new lease on life—and that's totally cool with me.

Just for fun I try on my prom dress tonight, along with the amazing shoes that I ordered online. They finally arrived this week and are absolutely perfect. I've never had a pair of real designer shoes before, but I got a great deal on these by ordering them from one of those overstock websites. They are none other than Prada, and while I really have no idea whether they're really "in style" or not, they were the perfect color of turquoise with high spike heels and lots of cool straps, and I happen to think they look fantastic. Plus they were really marked down. No way would I ever pay full price for something like designer shoes!

Even though Mom's already seen my shoes, she hasn't seen them with my dress, so I go and find her reading a magazine in the living room and give her a little "preview" show.

"Very glamorous," she tells me. "And are you wearing those earrings too?"

I reach up and touch my diamond studs. "Yeah, I thought they looked nice."

She smiles. "They look lovely."

Now my dad comes in and whistles the way dads do when their little girls are all dressed up. "I thought the prom was tomorrow."

"It is. This is just my dress rehearsal." Then I point out a shoe. "I hadn't actually seen my shoes with the dress yet."

"Very nice."

My mom clears her throat. "Oh, Allen. Is it okay if we give it to her early?"

Dad kind of laughs, and I immediately demand to know what "it" is.

"Well, since the cat's out of the bag..." He winks at Mom. "I'll be right back."

"I wasn't sure," she says to me with uncertainty. "I mean, you might've had something else, something, well...but I saw this in an ad, and I asked Dad to get it and..." She sighs. "Here he comes."

Dad comes in with a small velvet box that is obviously jewelry, and he hands it to Mom. "You give it to her."

"It's not just for the prom," she says. "It was also a congratulations gift for your column going into syndication. I thought since you have to keep that a secret, you could see this necklace and be reminded of it." Then she holds out the box for me to take.

I open it up to see a delicate gold necklace with three diamonds hanging in a vertical line. At least I think they are diamonds. "Is this real?" I ask with wide eyes.

Mom laughs. "Yes, of course, sweetheart. It's called an eternity necklace. One stone is for the past, one is for the present, and one is for the future. I thought it was a nice idea."

"It's beautiful." I carefully remove the necklace from the box. "I totally love it!" Then I sit on the couch beside Mom and wait as she clasps it around my neck.

"You're beautiful too, Kim." Then she kisses me on the cheek. "No one could ask for a better daughter."

Okay, this makes me cry, and I'm relieved that we did this the night BEFORE the prom since the idea of going to prom with puffy, red eyes isn't too appealing. We all hug and I thank them for it. "It's perfect," I tell them. "I hadn't really decided which necklace to wear, but this is perfect!"

Then we talk about the plans for tomorrow night, and I assure my parents that Matthew and I have planned in enough time to spend about twenty minutes with both sets of parents to ensure there are plenty of Kodak moments recorded.

"But you still don't know where he's taking you for

dinner yet?" asks Mom.

"No, but he promised me that I'd like it. And knowing Matthew it's probably something unique."

Mom smiles. "You're going to have so much fun, sweetheart."

"Yeah," I tell her. "I think so."

And I really do think so as I carefully hang up my dress then rewrap my shoes in tissue and replace my necklace back in its velvet box. And it makes it feel even better knowing that Mom's kind of rebounding. I could tell by the sparkle in her eyes and the tone of her voice that she's really feeling better. And I'm thinking, okay, maybe God really is healing her. Maybe we just needed to get this close to the edge just to realize how much we love her and need her.

I can hardly believe that she wants to go to the beauty salon with me tomorrow. But that's a really good sign too. And just seeing the old photos of Aunt Shannon and knowing that she lives in Beverly Hills makes me suspect that she's pretty high fashion, and I can understand how Mom doesn't want to be the older frumpy sister when Shannon gets here on Monday.

The only thing that keeps me from feeling totally happy tonight is knowing that, just down the street, my best friend is feeling perfectly miserable. I wish there was something I could do to cheer Nat up. I wonder if the counselor read my anonymous tip and made an appointment with her yet. But no way am I asking Nat about that. She'd probably chew my head off or maybe just hang up on me again or plant a homemade bomb in my bathroom.

Even so, I decide to e-mail her. Not that she's checking e-mail or ever responds these days, but I figure it's worth a shot.

Nat, hope you're feeling better. Remember that I'm here for you if you need to talk. And know that I love you and am praying for you. I know it must seem totally dark and miserable to you, but it's going to get better. Just ask God and I know He'll show you the light at the end of this tunnel. Trust Him; He won't let you down. Please, hang in there and call me if you want to talk. Or just come over. I miss my best friend! Love, Kim

Well, even though it's nearly eleven I'm still wide awake, probably in anticipation of tomorrow. So I e-mail Matthew and tell him my parents gave me a "gift" for the prom, but that's all—he'll have to wait to see it for himself. And knowing how much he likes my diamond stud earrings, I'm sure he'll think the necklace is pretty cool too.

Tomorrow is going to be the best. And since I'm still wide awake and don't have homework to do, I decide to get ahead on the Just Jamie letters. Especially since Aunt Shannon and Maya will be here on Monday. I'm sure I'll be wanting lots of free time to hang with them and hear all about this "famous" dude ex-husband and what their lives are like down in sunny Southern California.

Dear Jamie,

I just discovered that my older brother is using drugs. I confronted him, and he denied it, but I know for a fact that he is. My question is, what should I do? I hate being a narc, but I'm also really worried about him. I know my parents have no idea what's up. Help!

Little Sister

Dear Little Sister,

You say you "know for a fact" and you say you "confronted" him. If that's really true, then I think the next step is to talk to your parents. Drug use is serious and dangerous, and according to my research, the people who use drugs are the last ones to admit to it. Tell your parents. And don't feel like a narc when you do. The reason you'll tell your parents is because you love your brother and care about him. But your parents are in a much better position to deal with this. Good luck!

Just Jamie

Twenty-one

Sunday, April 30

The absolute best day of my life turned inside out last night. Nearly twenty-four hours later, I'm still trying to understand the whole thing. As tempting as it is to tell this whole thing backwards, I will try to record it chronologically—for the sake of my diary and my memories.

Yesterday, Mom and I went to Hyacinth, the surprisingly upscale salon where we both had appointments. There we were coifed and pampered. They even served us cucumber-flavored iced water, which was actually refreshing. Feeling very relaxed and lovely, I drove us home around one, and we both took a nap. Mom's nap lasted most of the afternoon, but I was up after less than an hour. I tried to make myself useful around the house since no hospice people come during the weekend. But at around five, I decided it was time to start getting ready for the Big Night.

Matthew showed up in the coolest old car, a mint condition Bentley from the fifties, that his grandma let him borrow (who knew he had a rich grandma?), and photos were taken, videos recorded, and both my parents thought Matthew's vintage tuxedo was strikingly handsome. And of course, I totally agreed. Then we went over to Matthew's house and posed as his mom took pictures and made a big deal over my dress.

"Prada shoes?" she exclaimed, and I told her what a bargain they were, and she commended me for my thriftiness. And then we were off to our dinner reservations, which happened to be at a new Japanese restaurant that just got rave reviews in the newspaper. (Matthew made reservations two weeks ago.)

Then we went to the prom, and it was more fun than I'd even imagined. Probably the most romantic evening of my life. Even so, I had no intention of heading off to the hotel like so many other couples were doing—like they think it was their wedding night, and they were going off to consummate their vows! Talk about stupid!

Anyway, Matthew knew that I didn't want to stay out too late, so he politely had me home just before midnight. As usual, we kissed at the door, and I told him it was the best night of my life and then said good night. Still feeling the lightheaded aftereffects of the prom, I sort of danced my way into the house and then immediately felt that something was wrong.

"Kim?"

"Who is it?" I asked then saw Natalie emerging from my kitchen. Her eyes were swollen and red, and I could tell she'd been crying.

"Do you need to talk?" I asked, certain that she'd finally come to her senses and decided to get help. Either that or she'd heard that Ben and Torrey were back together and had indeed made an appearance at the prom.

"It's your mom."

Now I felt confused, like someone had pulled a fast one on me. "What?"

"Your mom," she said in a very sober voice. Then she came over and put her arms around me. "She's gone."

"Gone?" I pulled away and glanced around the kitchen like I expected Mom to pop around the corner and offer us cocoa.

"She had a seizure." Nat helped me to sit down in a chair. "I heard the siren and looked out to see the ambulance pulling into your driveway. It was a little before eleven."

"No..."

"I came running over here to see what was wrong, and within minutes the paramedics were putting her into the ambulance. Your dad asked me to wait here for you since he knew you'd be home soon, and he wanted to follow the ambulance to—"

"She's at the hospital." I stood up. "I have to go."

"Your dad just called, Kim. He thought you might be home now."

"I am home."

"He wanted to—" she choked on the words. "He wanted you to know that she died, Kim."

"No!"

"I'm so sorry—"

I held up my cell phone. Matthew had just handed it back to me. It was still on. "Dad would've called me! I have my phone right here. See!"

"I'm sorry—"

"No! I'm getting my keys. I'm going to the hospital. She can't be dead, Nat. She just got her hair done. She's feeling better. Her sister's coming on Monday." I ran for my purse and dug for my keys.

"Here," Nat told me, taking my keys. "We'll both go to the hospital, but I'm driving."

I felt like I could barely breathe as Nat drove us to the hospital. My fingers were digging into the seat, and my ears were buzzing and ringing, and I felt like my chest was about to explode. Nat pulled up to the ER entrance, and I leaped out, running straight to the reception desk. "My mom is here!" I gasped. "Patricia Peterson!"

The woman was looking at her computer screen, taking forever, and I kept yelling at her, "Patricia Peterson! She just got here!"

Then I felt a hand on my shoulder and turned to see Dad's tear-streaked face looking at me with the saddest eyes I have ever seen. "We lost her, Kimmy."

I fell into his arms and just sobbed. I don't know how long we stood there, clinging to each other and crying. Finally I asked him if I could see her—like I needed to be convinced that she was really gone—and he led me back through ER and then opened the door to a dimly lit room.

My knees got weak as I looked at the bed. It was completely draped with a pale blue sheet. Dad slowly walked to the head of the bed and gently folded back the sheet so I could see her face, and I just stared in disbelief at the pale, motionless face.

"Mom," I formed the word, but no sound came out. Then I went closer and reached out to touch her cheek. Her skin was cool but smooth, almost wrinkle free, and for the first time in months she looked relaxed, free from pain. Tears were still sliding down my face as I reached to touch her hair. It still looked pretty, neatly cut and curled. "Oh, Mom," I gasped as reality slugged me in the gut. "I wish I'd been here," I sobbed. "I wish I could've said good-bye."

Dad put a hand on my shoulder again. "You did say good-bye, Kim. Right before you left for the prom. You kissed Mom and told her good-bye."

I took in a deep breath but didn't tell him that wasn't what I meant. That I wished I'd been here, by her side during her last moments. I would gladly have given up the prom, Matthew, everything just for that. But I didn't say anything to Dad. I didn't think I could form the words.

We found Nat in the waiting area, and she agreed to drive my Jeep home so I could ride with Dad. I didn't see how he could focus on driving, but somehow he managed. Maybe he was on automatic pilot, or maybe it was just that he'd made this trip (back and forth to the hospital) so many times before.

"I never really got to say good-bye to her either," he said after we were almost home.

"What do you mean?"

"She went to bed after you and Matthew left, said she just wanted to take a nap. But then she was sleeping so soundly, I couldn't bear to wake her. I was staying up, waiting for you to get home, and something made me decide to go check on her. I could tell something was wrong. She was awake and breathing but unable to talk. I called 9-1-1 and the next thing I knew, I was following the ambulance to the hospital. I kept telling myself it was going to be like last time. They would find what was wrong, fix it, and we'd come back home in the morning. But she was unconscious when I got to the hospital. She was hooked up to a respirator and all the machines, and they were working on her. But after about twenty minutes, she went into complete cardiac arrest, and they couldn't bring her back, Kim. She just died. I never did get to say good-bye."

I reached over and put my hand on his arm as he pulled into our driveway. "Mom knows how much you love her. She knows that we both love her. Maybe saying good-bye isn't such a big deal."

Then Nat pulled up, and Dad and I got out and stood in the driveway just looking at our house. And I know we were both thinking the same thing—it's going to be so empty without her.

And it is. I can't explain what it feels like exactly. As I walked around our house today, I imagined a house that had once been warmed by a big cheerful crackling fire—but then the fire was snuffed out, and the grate was cold and black. That's how our house feels now.

Neither of us went to church today. Maybe that was a mistake, but it's like we just didn't have it in us. We both just rambled around. Dad made phone calls, arrangements, and whatnot. I mostly felt lost and lonely. Even when Matthew called, it took me a minute to get my bearings. And then I told him, falling apart even before the words came out.

"I'm so sorry, Kim. Do you want me to come over?"

But I told him that it wasn't a good time and that I'd call him later. But I haven't. Not yet. Nat called too. She offered to come over, but again I declined. I mean, what good would it do?

Okay, I know that Mom's with God. I don't even have any doubts about that. But there is this big, painful hole, about the size of a football field, right in the center of my chest, and it hurts so bad that I don't think it will ever go away. And so, even though I know Mom is with God, I can't help but be mad at Him that she's not here with me. I mean, who needed her more? Me or God?

So instead of writing to Jamie for answers tonight, I am writing to God.

Dear God,

Why? Why? Why? Why did You have to take my mom? Would it have hurt You so much, or upset the order of the universe, if You'd let her stay just a little while longer? I don't get it, God. Dad and I still need her. There's no way You need her as much as we do. Why couldn't You have just let her live—even for just another week so she could meet her sister? I don't get it. Not only does it seem unfair, it seems unkind and unjust.

Kim

Then it occurs to me that Shannon probably doesn't even know about Mom's death yet. I never thought to ask Dad whether or not he called her today. I consider calling now, but it's so late. I'll have to remind Dad in the morning.

Monday, May 1

By the time I ask Dad about Shannon, he informs me it's too late. "They're probably at the airport by now, Kim. She'd booked an early morning flight that's supposed to get here around three, I think." He shakes his head. "I totally forgot about them."

"Does she have a cell phone?"

"If she does, I don't know the number."

"Maybe Mom wrote it down," I say. "I'll go look." Then I go into the bedroom, looking on the bed table next to her side of the bed. I find her little notebook where she makes her lists and whatnot, the place where she might jot down a phone number. But I don't see anything. However, I do see two envelopes tucked into the back of the notebook. One has my name on the front; the other is for my dad. I go out to where he is making a pot of coffee and hold them up. "Have you seen these?"

He studies them for a moment then shakes his head.

"They were in the back of Mom's little notebook."

We both take our letters and go off to separate places to read them. I go out to the porch and sit in Mom's favorite wicker rocker, carefully unsealing the envelope and removing the pages.

Dear Kim,

If you are reading this letter, I must be gone. To say I know how you feel is rather presumptuous on my part, but I do remember how I felt when I lost my mother so many years ago. It's something you never forget. And although I am tired and my body is failing me now, I would give anything to stay here with you—to watch you graduate from high school (with honors!) and then college (with even more honors!) and to see you launched into some impressive career (probably with even more honors!) and then one day to see you walk down the aisle with your true love and then later on to bounce a grandbaby on my knee. Oh, what I would give to be there for all those events with you.

Sweet Kim, you have been the most precious gift in my life. When I realized that I was unable to bear children, I believed that God had another plan. And He did! I will never forget the day we picked you up at the orphanage in Seoul. You were only six months old, and you were already sitting up—and those big dark eyes were so alert, so wise! We knew from the start that you were a special child. I instantly fell in love with you, sweetheart. And my love for you has only grown over the years.

I'm sorry that I can't physically be with you anymore. But I have this deep sense, this blessed assurance, that I'll be able to check in on you from time to time—like when you graduate or marry or have children... Goodness, it wouldn't be heaven if I were cut off from my two loved ones permanently, now would it? So please know that although I am away, I am still here. My love for you will go on forever. And eventually we will all be together again. I believe that with my whole heart. In the meantime, we will just do our best, won't we? And knowing you, my Kim, you will do better than your best—you always do.

Now here is my final wish for you, sweetheart. It's something I've never really put into words but have always wanted to say: Take time to breathe, to feel the sun on your head, to smell the roses, and to laugh. You've always been a serious girl, but don't forget to have fun, to appreciate the goodness all around you, and to hear the birds singing in the trees. Those are all God's gifts to you, and I want you to enjoy them—and to enjoy the wonderful life that is stretched out before you! And when you do those things, my sweet daughter, remember me!

Love always and forever,

Mom

More tears are running down my cheeks now. I wonder if they will ever stop and then suddenly I hear something—a bird singing from the maple tree in the front yard. I remember what Mom wrote about listening to the birds. And so I just sit and listen. And quite honestly, it's the first time I actually recall just sitting still and listening to a bird like that. And it's the most beautiful thing I've ever heard.

For a moment my old Buddhist ways return, and I

actually wonder if it's Mom, in the form of a bird, singing to me. Then I remember what she said about the sun on my head, so I go out and stand in the yard. I feel its sharp warmth on my dark hair, and it actually feels pretty good. Then I see all the flowers that I planted for Mom over a month ago. At the time they were kind of scrawny and spindly with very few blooms, but today they are a rainbow of color and blossoms. Why hadn't I even noticed them before?

"Thanks, Mom," I say with my face to the sky.

Tuesday, May 2

Aunt Shannon and Maya arrived yesterday afternoon. Dad and I met them at the airport, holding up a sign that simply said, "Shannon and Maya," because the truth is, we don't even know their last name. Fortunately they spotted us standing just outside of the baggage claim area; fortunate because I seriously doubt that we ever would've recognized them. But they came, lugging their bags, the older one waving to us and pointing at the sign.

It turns out that Aunt Shannon is no longer a brunette (like in her teen pictures). She's a very thin, fast-talking, stylishly dressed blonde. The first thing she did after getting outside the terminal was to light up a cigarette. "I thought I was going to die for the lack of a smoke," she said after she took in a long drag.

"I'm Allen Peterson," my dad told her. "This is Kim."

She smiled and shook our hands. "I'm Shannon and this is Maya."

Now Maya's the one who took me slightly by surprise with her olive-toned skin and long, dark, curly hair. Other than being head-turning gorgeous, she doesn't look anything like her mother. But being Korean with Caucasian parents I'm used to being "different," so I don't say anything. Neither does Dad.

As we walked to the car, Aunt Shannon kept talking almost nonstop about the crummy flight, bad food, poor service, and air turbulence. "I don't know why they even bother to call it first class anymore. They load everyone in like cattle these days. And security, well, don't even get me going."

Finally, we were in the car. Aunt Shannon in front with Dad, and me in the backseat with Maya, who didn't look very pleased to be here.

Dad cleared his throat, and I could hear it coming. "Uh, Shannon, I need to tell you something... We would've called, but everything happened so quickly, and then we were busy and, well, somewhat distracted...but Patricia passed away quite late on Saturday night."

"Oh, no!" Aunt Shannon shrieked so loudly that I nearly jumped out of my seat. "Oh, please, Allen, tell me it's not true. Patricia died?"

"I wish it weren't true—" his voice broke slightly. "But it is. Kim and I have been pretty devastated. We would've called, but we were both—"

"Oh, I can't believe it. I can't believe after all these years...and being so close...I can't believe I missed her." And then she started crying, sobbing loudly.

I was sitting directly behind her, so I put my hand on her shoulder. "Mom really wanted to see you," I told her. "I thought maybe it was helping her to hang on—she'd been feeling so badly before the phone call. And then she rallied, didn't she, Dad?"

He nodded. "She was so happy to hear your voice, Shannon. So glad that you were alive and doing well."

Aunt Shannon blew her nose. "This is just my luck!"

"Oh, Mom," Maya said with clear exasperation. "This isn't about you."

"She was my sister, Maya! It most certainly is about me."

And to my shock and horror, they got into this huge argument right there in the car as Dad drove us home. They said horrible things to each other and even used profanity. I couldn't even imagine what Dad was thinking, but I was totally shocked.

By the time we pulled into the driveway, they'd finally settled down, and I thought that they might apologize to us for their complete lack of manners or discretion, but they didn't.

"Is this your house?" asked Shannon. (At this point I had decided not to call her "Aunt" Shannon any longer.)

"This is our humble abode," said my dad. The apologetic tone to his voice irritated me. I mean, what reason do we have to be sorry about anything—well, other than losing Mom?

"I thought you were the managing editor of a big newspaper?" she said as Dad unloaded their bags.

"It's just the local paper," my dad told her. "Small potatoes."

We helped them get their bags into the "humble abode" and to their room.

"We're sharing a room?" Maya said, more to her mother than to us since we'd already gone out.

I gave Dad a questioning glance, and he just shrugged as if he didn't even care. Then I heard more arguing and the discussion of one or both of them going to a hotel. I, personally, am voting for the hotel!

Their arguing seems to be a fairly nonstop thing. It gives me a headache and makes my dad create excuses to leave. Instead of going to a hotel, Maya has opted to sleep on the couch in the family room. I would've offered to share my room with her, but she kind of scares me. In fact, the only reason I'm nice to them at all is because of Mom. They are, after all, her relatives.

Tonight, Dad and I take a little walk. Mostly to escape another argument between the two of them.

"It's hard to believe they're related to Mom," I say once we're a few houses away.

He sighs deeply. "I know..."

"It occurred to me that they're her actual flesh and blood relatives, and I'm not."

Well, Dad stops right in the middle of the sidewalk,

reaches over and takes both my hands, and says, "Kim Patricia Peterson, if you're not your mom's flesh and blood, then no one is. You are more like your mom than Shannon or Maya will ever be. And don't you ever forget it."

I nod without saying anything. Although it was a little abrupt, I know that Dad was paying me the highest compliment possible, and I will NEVER forget it.

"What are we going to do about them?" I finally ask as we turn to head back. I don't admit to Dad that I've been secretly calling them Paris Hilton and Nicole Ritchie since they seem about that spoiled and inconsiderate.

He just shrugs. "Don't know that there's much we can do, Kim. We'll be hospitable for your mom's sake; they'll come to her funeral, and then hopefully go home the next day. I asked Shannon if she'd been able to rearrange their return flight, and she said she was working on it."

"Dad?" I say as we're getting closer to our house.

"Yeah?"

"Do you think it was kind of a blessing for Mom to go before she actually met them in person?"

Now for the first time since losing Mom, Dad almost laughs. Then he reaches over and puts his arm around my shoulders and pulls me toward him. "Maybe so, Kimmy. Maybe so."

And so that's what I'm thinking. I mean, knowing Mom and how much she was looking forward to seeing Shannon and meeting her only niece, I think it would've hurt her deeply to see the way they treat each other, to hear their arguments and how they swear at each other like drunken sailors.

Mom had a sweet and sensitive spirit, and I think seeing her own flesh and blood carrying on like this would've just killed her. And if Mom had to die, I'd much rather she died peacefully in her sleep than in the midst of such open hatred and bitterness. So maybe God did know what He was doing after all.

Twenty-two

Wednesday, May 3

Mom's funeral was sweet and simple, probably exactly what she wanted. It was held at my parents' church, which was packed to standing room only. I was surprised at how many people came—and even more surprised at how each of them (at least the ones who spoke to me) really knew and loved her. I couldn't believe how many people said that Mom had done something to help or encourage them at some point in their lives. I mean, here I thought she spent most of her time at home just doing laundry or baking cookies, and she had this whole other life of helping others. Go figure.

I was also surprised to see how many of my friends from school and church were there. It's almost like I'd forgotten all about these people during the past several days. But apparently they haven't forgotten me. Even Chloe, Laura, and Allie were there. I hadn't even heard they were back from tour. And Pastor Tony and his wife were there, along with Josh Miller and his fiancée, Caitlin.

"I'm so sorry," Caitlin told me when we went downstairs after the service.

I nodded. "Yeah, I know." Then I thought of something. "You remember when you asked me about playing 'Ave Maria'?"

"Yes." She frowned. "But I'll totally understand if you changed your mind, Kim. I mean, you've been through—"

"No, that's not it. I just wanted to tell you how ironic it was that you wanted that piece since my mom had loved it and I learned it last December just so I could play it for her at Christmas."

Caitlin got tears in her eyes then hugged me. "That's awesome, Kim. I wish I'd known your mom."

"You would've liked her."

And that's what I thought as we stood by her grave later this afternoon. Everyone liked her. I honestly couldn't think of one single person who didn't like my mom. And then I asked myself why was that so—I mean, I know there are people who don't like me, but then I don't especially like them either—and that's when it occurred to me that it was because my mom liked everyone. She was the kind of person who could find the good in anyone. No matter who I brought home, what they looked like, what their family was like, Mom always liked and accepted them. Now some people may think that's no big deal, but to me it was totally amazing!

But in the same moment that this revelation hit me, I glanced over to where Shannon and Maya were standing off to one side. While I know that Mom totally loved her sister, it occurred to me that she'd never met her niece, Maya. And watching Maya standing there with her scowling face and narrowed eyes, with her arms folded tightly across her chest like she could hardly stand us and couldn't wait to get out of here and back to her fashionable friends in Beverly Hills, it hit me—Mom would've loved her too!

So now I'm back home, and I realize that Mom's not here anymore, and that it's up to me to love someone as unlovable as Maya. As it turns out, "Paris and Nicole's" airline tickets are nonrefundable, and their return flight isn't scheduled until next Wednesday. So it looks like God is giving me one whole week to practice loving someone in the same way my mom would've done.

God help me, I hope I'm up to it!

Reader's Guide

1. Kim seemed to have a good relationship with her mother. Why do you think that was? In what ways can your relationship with your mother be improved?

2. How do you think you'd feel if someone close to you was dying? Describe the emotions you might experience.

3. Natalie had really been on Kim to "be careful" in her relationship with Matthew. Why do you think she was so pushy about this?

4. Do you think that Christians should date unbelievers? Why or why not?

5. Were you surprised to learn that Natalie and Benjamin had had sex? Why or why not?

6. If you were Natalie, what could someone say to you that would help you to feel better and move on?

7. Why do you think Nat is having such a hard time talking to God?

8. Do you think Kim is finished grieving for her mother? What would you say to her if you were her friend?

9. Shannon and Maya seem to have some issues. How do you think Kim will handle them staying in their home for another week?

10. What do you think the future holds for Kim and Matthew? If you were Kim's friend, what would you tell her about this relationship?

Diary of a Teenage Girl Series

Enter Kim's World

JUST ASK, Kim book one

"Blackmailed" to regain driving privileges, Kim Peterson agrees to anonymously write a teen advice column for her dad's newspaper. No big deal, she thinks, until she sees her friends' heartaches in bold black and white. Suddenly Kim knows she does NOT have all the answers and is forced to turn to the One who does.

ISBN 1-59052-321-0

MEANT TO BE, Kim book two

Hundreds of people pray for the healing of Kim's mother. As her mother improves, Kim's relationship with Matthew develops. Natalie thinks it's wrong for a Christian to date a non-Christian. But Nat's dating life isn't exactly smooth sailing, either. Both girls are praying a lot—and waiting to find out what's meant to be.

ISBN 1-59052-322-9

FALLING UP, Kim book three *(Available February 2006)*

It's summer, and Kim is overwhelmed by difficult relatives, an unpredictable boyfriend, and a best friend who just discovered she's pregnant. Kim's stress level increases until a breakdown forces her to take a vacation. How will she get through these troubling times without going crazy?

ISBN 1-59052-324-5

THAT WAS THEN..., Kim book four *(Available June 2006)*

Kim starts her senior year with big faith and big challenges ahead. Her best friend is pregnant and believes it's God's will that she marry the father. But Kim isn't so sure. Then she receives a letter from her birth mom who wants to meet her, which rocks Kim's world. Can her spiritual maturity make a difference in the lives of those around her?

ISBN 1-59052-425-X

Diary of a Teenage Girl Series

Caitlin

Check Out More Great Fiction by Melody Carlson

***DIARY OF A TEENAGE GIRL*, Caitlin book one**

Follow sixteen-year-old Caitlin O'Conner as she makes her way through life—surviving a challenging home life, school pressures, an identity crisis, and the uncertainties of "true love." You'll cry with Caitlin as she experiences heartache, and cheer for her as she encounters a new reality in her life: God. See how rejection by one group can—incredibly—sometimes lead you to discover who you really are.

ISBN 1-57673-735-7

***IT'S MY LIFE*, Caitlin book two**

Caitlin faces new trials as she strives to maintain the recent commitments she's made to God. Torn between new spiritual directions and loyalty to Beanie, her pregnant best friend, Caitlin searches out her personal values on friendship, dating, life goals, and family.

ISBN 1-59052-053-X

***WHO I AM*, Caitlin book three**

As a high school senior, Caitlin's relationship with Josh takes on a serious tone via e-mail—threatening her commitment to "kiss dating good-bye." When Beanie begins dating an African-American, Caitlin's concern over dating seems to be misread as racism. One thing is obvious: God is at work through this dynamic girl in very real but puzzling ways, and a soul-stretching time of racial reconciliation at school and within her church helps her discover God's will as never before.

ISBN 1-57673-890-6

***ON MY OWN*, Caitlin book four**

An avalanche of emotion hits Caitlin as she lands at college and begins to realize she's not in high school anymore. Buried in coursework and far from her best friend, Beanie, Caitlin must cope with her new roommate's bad attitude, manic music, and sleazy social life. Should she have chosen a Bible college like Josh? Maybe...but how to survive the year ahead is the big question right now!

ISBN 1-59052-017-3

***I DO*, Caitlin book five**

Caitlin, now 21 and in her senior year of college, accepts Josh Miller's proposal for marriage. But Caitlin soon discovers there's a lot more to getting married than just saying "I do." Between her mother, mother-in-law to be, and Caitlin's old buddies, Caitlin's life never seems to run smoothly. As a result, the journey to her wedding is full of twists and turns where God touches many lives, including her own.

ISBN 1-59052-320-2

Diary of a Teenage Girl Series

Chloe

Diaries Are a Girl's Best Friend

MY NAME IS CHLOE, Chloe book one

Chloe Miller, Josh's younger sister, is a free spirit with dramatic clothes and hair. She struggles with her identity, classmates, parents, boys, and whether or not God is for real. But this unconventional high school freshman definitely doesn't hold back when she meets Him in a big, personal way. Chloe expresses God's love and grace through the girl band, Redemption, that she forms, and continues to show the world she's not willing to conform to anyone else's image of who or what she should be. Except God's, that is.

ISBN 1-59052-018-1

SOLD OUT, Chloe book two

Chloe and her fellow band members must sort out their lives as they become a hit in the local community. And after a talent scout from Nashville discovers the trio, all too soon their explosive musical ministry begins to encounter conflicts with family, so-called friends, and school. Exhilarated yet frustrated, Chloe puts her dream in God's hand and prays for Him to work out the details.

ISBN 1-59052-141-2

ROAD TRIP, Chloe book three

After signing with a major record company, Redemption's dreams are coming true. Chloe, Allie, and Laura begin their concert tour with the good-looking guys in the band Iron Cross. But as soon as the glitz and glamour wear off, the girls find life on the road a little overwhelming. Even rock-solid Laura appears to be feeling the stress—and Chloe isn't quite sure how to confront her about the growing signs of drug addiction...

ISBN 1-59052-142-0

FACE THE MUSIC, Chloe book four

Redemption has made it to the bestseller chart, but what Chloe and the girls need most is some downtime to sift through the usual high school stress with grades, friends, guys, and the prom. Chloe struggles to recover from a serious crush on the band leader of Iron Cross. Then just as an unexpected romance catches Redemption by surprise, Caitlin O'Conner—whose relationship with Josh is taking on a new dimension—joins the tour as a chaperone. Chloe's wild ride only speeds up, and this one-of-a-kind musician faces the fact that life may never be normal again.

ISBN 1-59052-241-9

Here's a sneak peek of Kim's next diary—*Falling Up* —

Thursday, May 4

I woke up crying last night. Sobbing so hard my chest hurt. I thought it was a nightmare, although I couldn't recall anything specific. Only this heaviness pressing down on me like a bag of rocks, like my world had come to a horrible end. I tried to shake it off, the way I used to do as a child after a frightening dream. Or else I'd sneak off to my parents' room, crawling into bed with them, always on my mom's side, snuggling up to her and sometimes even warming my cold feet on her. She never once complained.

And then I remembered...<u>Mom is gone</u>. Like a slap in the face I remembered that she had died on Saturday night, prom night, and that her funeral service had been just yesterday. Full realization hit me—<u>my mom is gone, and she isn't coming back</u>! That's when I started crying all over again. Only harder now. How long will it take for this to really sink in? And how long until that dull ache deep down inside of me goes away?

This morning I get out of bed and start to leave my room when I remember that Maya and Aunt Shannon are still here. Maya is sleeping in the family room, and I might wake her up if I go tiptoeing around. And after my last "interaction" with her yesterday afternoon, well, I'm not eager to disturb her and set myself up for another big mess. So I sit at my computer and catch up my diary. Or so I think. Mostly I've been sitting here, staring at the blank screen and wishing that this ache would go away. I so miss my mom.

"At least you had a good mom," Maya said yesterday afternoon, after I accidentally stumbled upon her sitting in a chaise lounge on the back deck. I'd gone out there to get away from Shannon, who was sitting like a hypnotized stone in front of the blaring TV, watching some ridiculous soap opera that she's addicted to since she actually had a small role on it back in the early eighties.

"Huh?" I said as I tried to decide how to gracefully exit. I could pretend that I came out here to get something, but what?

"Or so it seems," she added with a dramatic roll of her dark brown eyes. Maya is astonishingly beautiful, the kind of girl who people actually stop and stare at.

Realizing that there was no polite way to escape my cranky cousin and remembering my resolution to honor my mother by being kind to her relatives, I decided to sit in the lounge chair next to Maya. At least it was quieter out here. I leaned back and sighed. But I still didn't respond to her comment about our moms. I knew better than to engage by now.

"It's true," she continued, as if looking for an argument, which wasn't surprising. "I can hardly believe that your mom and my mom were actually sisters. It's like your mom was some sort of saint, and my mom," she laughed an evil sort of laugh, "is the devil."

"Your mom's not the devil."

"Like you'd even know."

"Maybe not. Still, I'm guessing that this whole thing is pretty upsetting to her, I mean, making the trip out here after all these years, and then she finds out she's too late to see her only sister. Well, she's got to be feeling pretty bummed, don't you think?"

Maya turned around and stared at me, her expression was that of an experienced grown-up looking down on a sadly misinformed child. "See, that's just how much you don't get it, Kim. You have absolutely no idea what you're talking about. This is the story of Shannon's life—a day late and a dollar short. It's just the way that woman operates."

I had no idea how to respond to that, so I changed the subject. "You know, my mom told me that Shannon had been married to someone famous, but with all that's been going on...well, I totally forgot to ask who it was."

"Don't bother."

"Why?" I asked.

"Because it's inconsequential."

"Inconsequential to whom?"

"To you or me or anyone."

I considered this. "So, is this inconsequential person your dad?"

She rolled her eyes again then picked up an old magazine on the table between us. She pretended to be interested as she flipped through its slightly curled pages, but I seriously doubted that "Good Housekeeping" was that engaging to someone like her.

Then she abruptly set the magazine back down. "If you really must know, this inconsequential person is my dad." She stared at me with those incredible eyes, her perfectly arched brows pulled together in a fierce frown. "Satisfied now?"

"Not completely. I'm still curious as to whether or not he's famous. Like is he someone I would know?"

She just pressed her lips together, shaking her head as a sigh escaped. So dramatic. Sometimes I find it hard to believe this girl is only fifteen. "Oh, if you must know...Have you ever heard of Nick Stark?"

"You mean the singer Nick Stark?"

"Yeah, the old Nick Stark has-been performer from the swinging seventies I've-seen-better-days pop singer."

"He's not exactly a has-been, Maya." I felt slightly embarrassed to hear the excitement in my voice growing, like I was some kind of Nick Stark groupie, which I am not. "I thought Nick was making a comeback. I mean, he did the soundtrack for that hit movie last year—what was it called? The one with Denzel Washington and what's her name?"

"Yeah, yeah," Maya said with a bored expression. "His supposedly big comeback. One movie. Big deal."

"But aren't you proud of him?"

She just shrugged.

Then it occurred to me that since Shannon and Nick were divorced, perhaps Maya wasn't too involved in her dad's life. "Do you see much of him?"

She laughed. "Yeah, right."

"So he's not around much?" I tried to inject some sympathy into my voice.

"Not if Shannon has anything to say about it. Other than sending his monthly check, Nick keeps a pretty low profile in our neighborhood. She makes sure of that."

"They don't get along?"

"Like oil and water, cats and dogs, whatever cliché you can think of. They are a restraining order or prison sentence waiting to happen. My mom actually keeps a gun under her pillow."

"Is she really afraid of him?"

"Afraid?" Maya looked like she was going to laugh again. "Yeah, right. She keeps the gun just hoping he'll show up some night, and she can pretend he's a prowler and blow his head off. That's how much she hates him."

"Oh."

"Yes, that must seem very strange and foreign to someone as protected as you." Maya looked thoroughly disgusted now. "You live out here in middle America with your happy little family in your happy little neighborhood just like some freakin' family sitcom. So totally unreal!" She stood up and stormed away.

And I know it was stupid for me to even react. I mean, why should I care about what someone like Maya thinks? Talk about needing a reality check! "Happy little family?" We just lost Mom for Pete's sake!

I really wish Maya and Shannon would go home. I'm

tempted to take money out of my own savings to help them change their tickets so they can be out of our hair and our home for good. But then, what would Mom do? What would she want?

So after I cooled off, I reconsidered the news that Nick Stark is like my uncle, or sort of, and I got to thinking that it was kind of interesting. So I do a little investigating of Nick Stark online. And it turns out, I was right; he is making a serious comeback in his singing career.

But here's what makes me sort of sad. I just realized how Mom would've gotten such a big kick out of this news. It's just the kind of thing she would've called up a good friend and enjoyed a good chat over. I wouldn't even be surprised if my parents have some old Nick Stark records stashed away someplace. But then she's not here to have fun with it. She never even had the chance to find out about her famous "relative."

On second thought, she might not have liked all the family feuding that comes with getting to know our "extended" family. And she'd probably feel sad to learn that Shannon is so bitter about her ex and that she and Maya are always at such odds.

Still, I think she would've gotten a kick out of a famous brother-in-law. Even if he is an ex. But maybe she's well aware of all this by now. I mean, wouldn't God let her in on all these sorts of interesting developments up in heaven? Or maybe no one cares about stuff like that up there. Who knows? It's too much for my little brain to think about. Especially at 3:14 A.M.